THE
HOCHSTETLER
STORY

THE
HOCHSTETLER
STORY

With photographs, maps, and historical background

ERVIN R. STUTZMAN

Herald Press
Harrisonburg, Virginia
Kitchener, Ontario

Library of Congress Cataloging-in-Publication Data
as it appears in *Jacob's Choice: Expanded Edition*
Stutzman, Ervin R., 1953-
  Jacob's choice / Ervin R. Stutzman. -- Expanded edition with photo-
graphs, maps, and historical background.
    pages cm. -- (Return to Northkill ; bk. 1)
    Includes bibliographical references.
    ISBN 978-0-8361-9875-1 (hardcover : alk. paper) 1. Amish--Fiction. I.
Title.
    PS3619.T88J33 2014
    813'.6--dc23

                        2013041014

THE HOCHSTETLER STORY
Copyright © 2015 by Herald Press, Harrisonburg, Virginia 22802
Released simultaneously in Canada by Herald Press,
Waterloo, Ontario N2L 6H7. All rights reserved.
International Standard Book Number: 978-1-5138-0037-0
Jacob's Choice: Expanded Edition ISBN Number: 978-0-8361-9875-1 (HC)
Jacob's Choice ISBN Number: 978-0-8361-9681-8 (PB)
Printed in United States of America
Cover design and layout by Reuben Graham

Unless otherwise noted, Scripture text is quoted, with permission, from
the King James Version.

To order or request information, please call 1-800-245-7894
or visit www.heraldpress.com.

19 18 17 16 15   10 9 8 7 6 5 4 3 2 1

To Rachel Weaver Kreider, the centenarian whose unflagging energy, irenic spirit, scrupulous Amish genealogical scholarship, and interest in the Jacob Hochstetler family story inspire me to follow in her footsteps, although I hardly dare hope to live as long as she has.

Contents

Historical Background

Jacob Hochstetler's family was but one of thousands in colonial Pennsylvania whose lives were shattered by the events of the French and Indian War. The Seven Years' War, as it is often called, was international in scope, encompassing eleven nations on four continents. Scholars have documented the immense legacy of this clash of empires, which forever altered the social and religious landscape of America.

It would be difficult to overestimate the significance of two developments in the aftermath of the conflict. One was the forcible and widespread displacement of Native American peoples and disruption of their way of life. The other was the levying of taxes to pay for the war's expenses, which, among other vexations, provoked the colonists to revolt and eventually establish the United States of America.

The account of Jacob Hochstetler's experiences was first written as an essay by William F. Hochstetler as part of the introduction to Harvey Hostetler's massive genealogy book listing the descendants of Jacob Hochstetler and his first wife, whose name remains unknown. The 1912 edition lists 9,197 families, largely descendants of Jacob's three sons who survived the attack.

In 1938, Harvey Hostetler printed an even larger genealogical record of the descendants of Jacob's daughter, Barbara Stutzman, listing 15,550 families. Amish families are generally aware of their genealogical ancestry; their shelves often house several books tracing their ancestral lineage through various family lines.

Descendants of Jacob Hochstetler formed the Jacob Hochstetler Family Association, Inc. in 1988, which publishes the quarterly *Hochstetler/Hostetler/Hochstedler (H/H/H) Family Newsletter*. Historical researchers regularly publish their family research in the newsletter, including articles with corrections to William Hochstetler's account.

Online genealogical databases now make it possible for many people to quickly determine if they are a descendant of the Hochstetler clan, and if so, their relationship to their thousands of cousins. Because marriages to relatives within the Amish community are common, many people can trace their lineage directly to Jacob Hochstetler by several different paths, at times through all four of his children who had descendants—Barbara, John, Joseph, and Christian.

One serious downside of the close intermarriage among Jacob's descendants is the occurrence of two peculiar forms of dwarfism among the Amish that have been traced by gene studies directly to Jacob Hochstetler and a neighbor, John Miller. Geneticists have suggested that the two men may have been in-laws with a near common ancestor who carried the gene that produces this genetic malady.

The most visible public reminder of the story of Jacob Hochstetler is a Pennsylvania Historical and Museum Commission marker located just south of Interstate 78 near Shartlesville, Pennsylvania. It sits right next to old Route 22, where the road runs behind a Roadside America Inn. The sign says: "The first organized Amish Mennonite congregation in America. Established by 1740. Disbanded following Indian attack, September 29, 1757, in which a Provincial soldier and three members of the Jacob Hochstetler family were killed near this point." Although not entirely true to fact, it stands as silent testimony to a significant era in the spiritual landscape of the land we call America.

Photographs

Northkill Creek

House built on site of Indian attack on Hochstetler family

Site of Buckaloons Seneca Indian village

Confluence of Brokenstraw Creek and Allegheny River at Buckaloons

Historical marker for Jacob Hertzler home

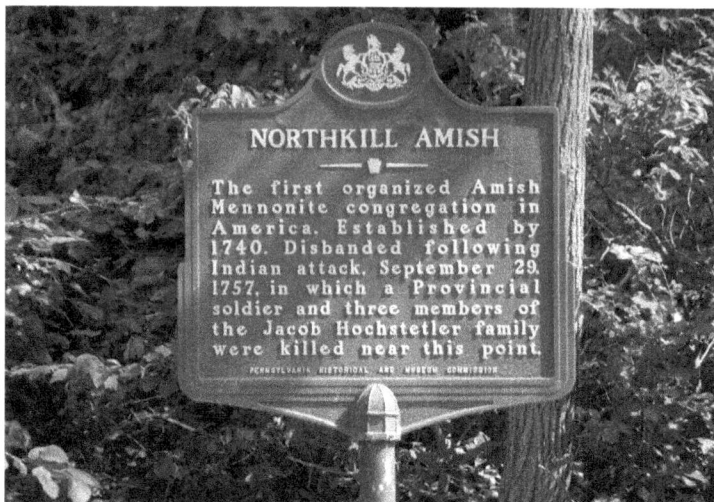

Historical marker of Indian attack on Hochstetler family

Historical marker for Fort Augusta

Maps

Map 1: Jacob Hochstetler Homestead

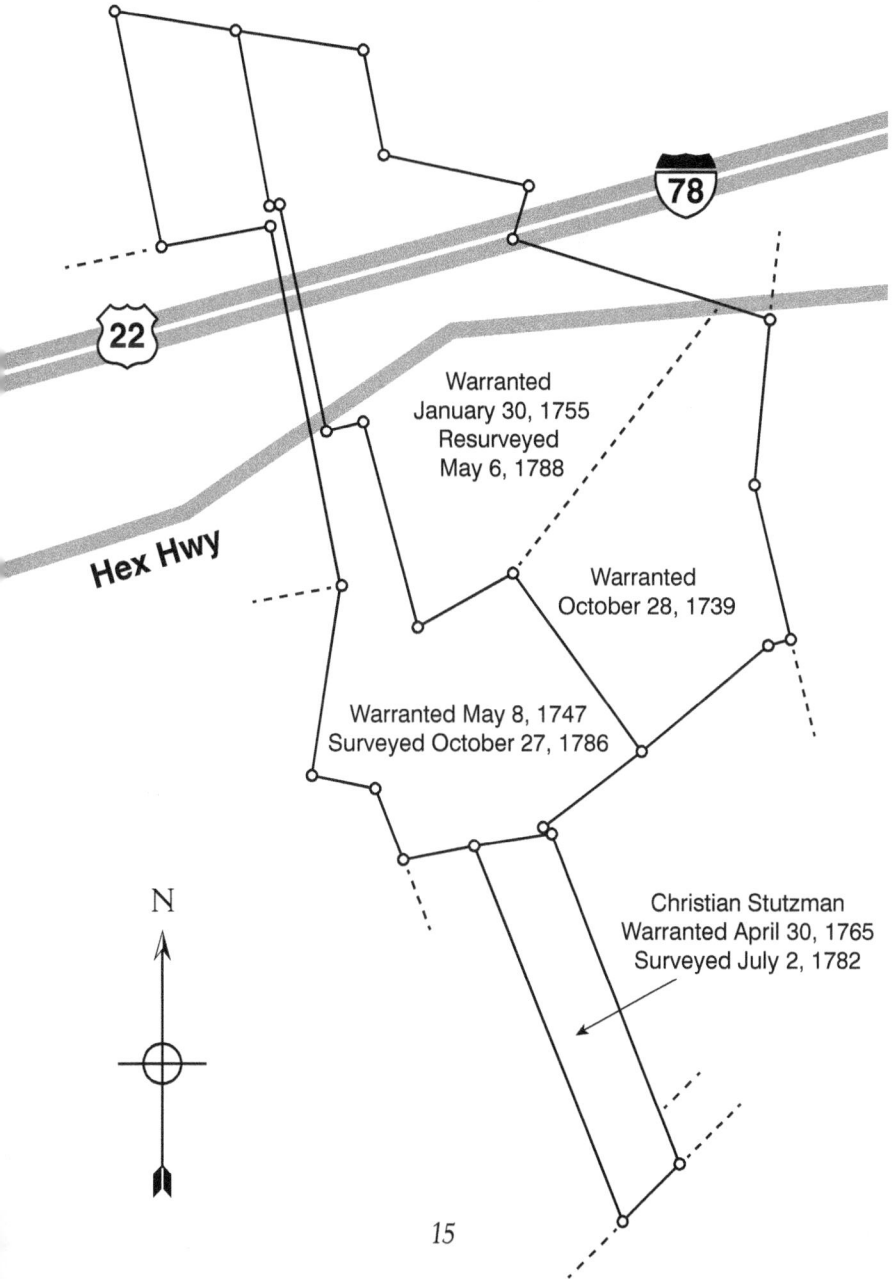

78

22

Warranted
January 30, 1755
Resurveyed
May 6, 1788

Hex Hwy

Warranted
October 28, 1739

Warranted May 8, 1747
Surveyed October 27, 1786

N

Christian Stutzman
Warranted April 30, 1765
Surveyed July 2, 1782

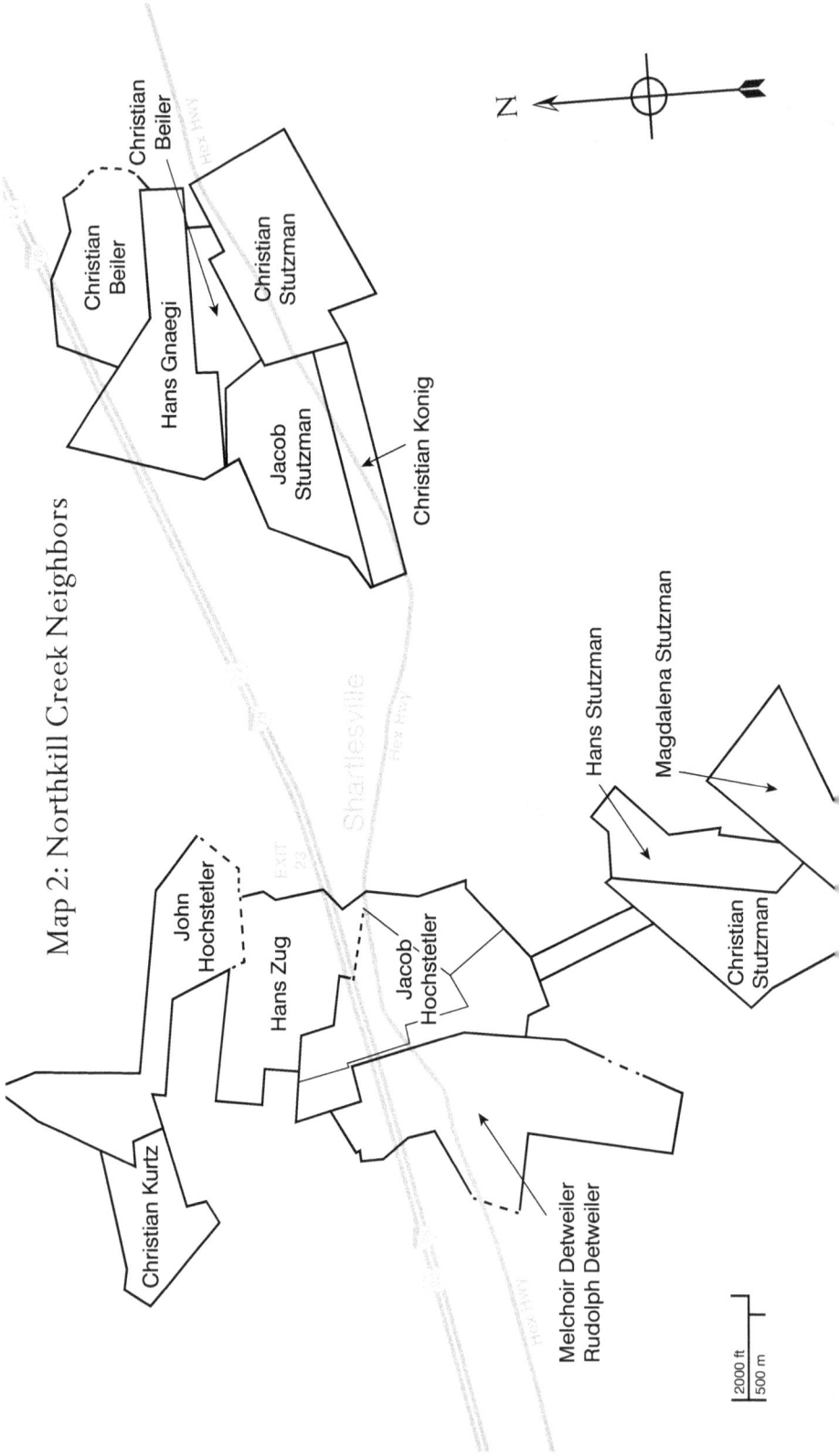

Map 2: Northkill Creek Neighbors

Christian Beiler
Christian Beiler
Christian Beiler
Hans Gnaegi
Christian Stutzman
Jacob Stutzman
Christian Konig

Hans Stutzman
Magdalena Stutzman
Christian Stutzman

John Hochstetler
Hans Zug
Christian Kurtz
Jacob Hochstetler
Melchoir Detweiler
Rudolph Detweiler

Shartlesville

N

2000 ft
500 m

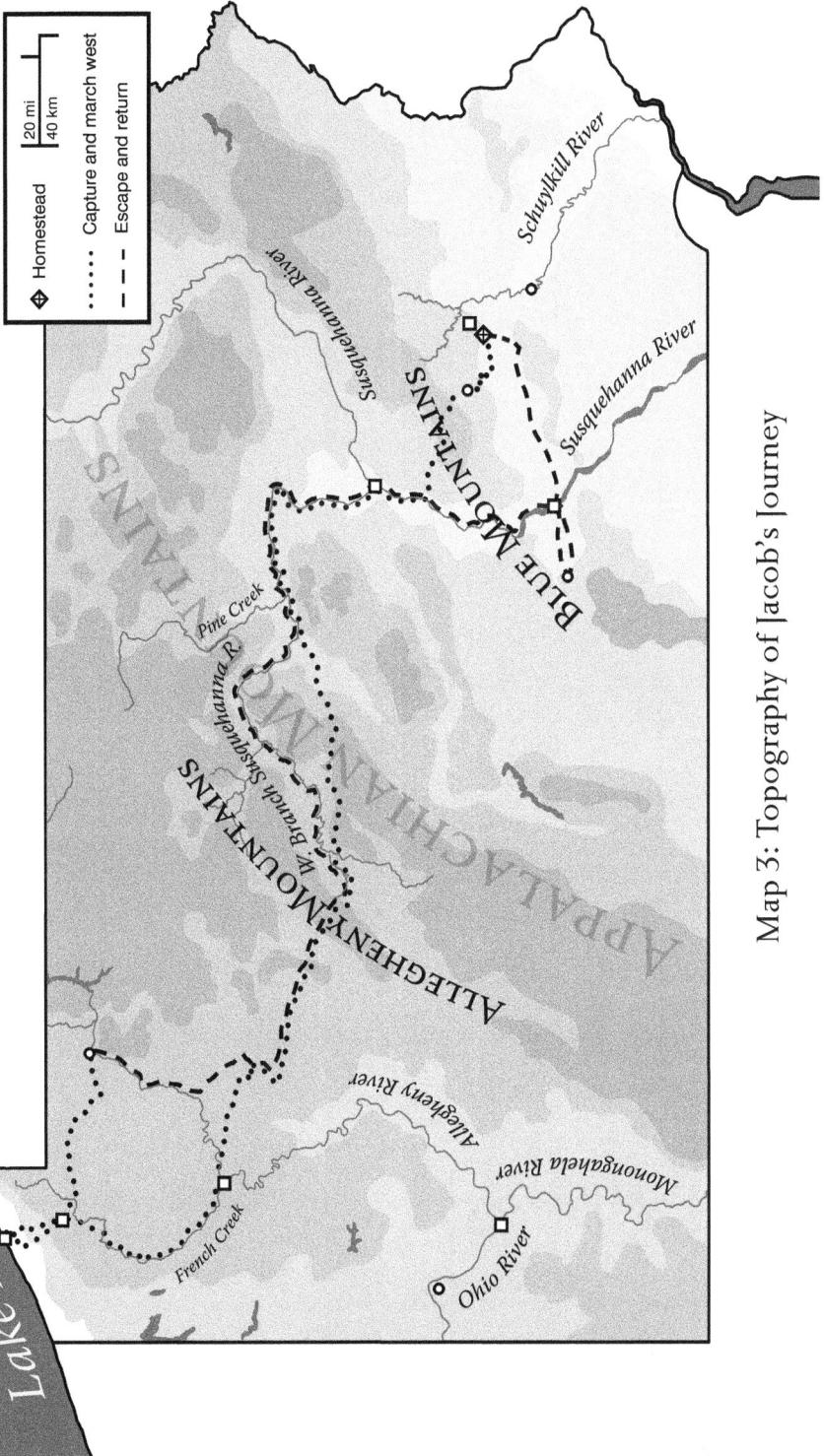

Map 3: Topography of Jacob's Journey

Map 4: Historical Locations along Jacob's Route

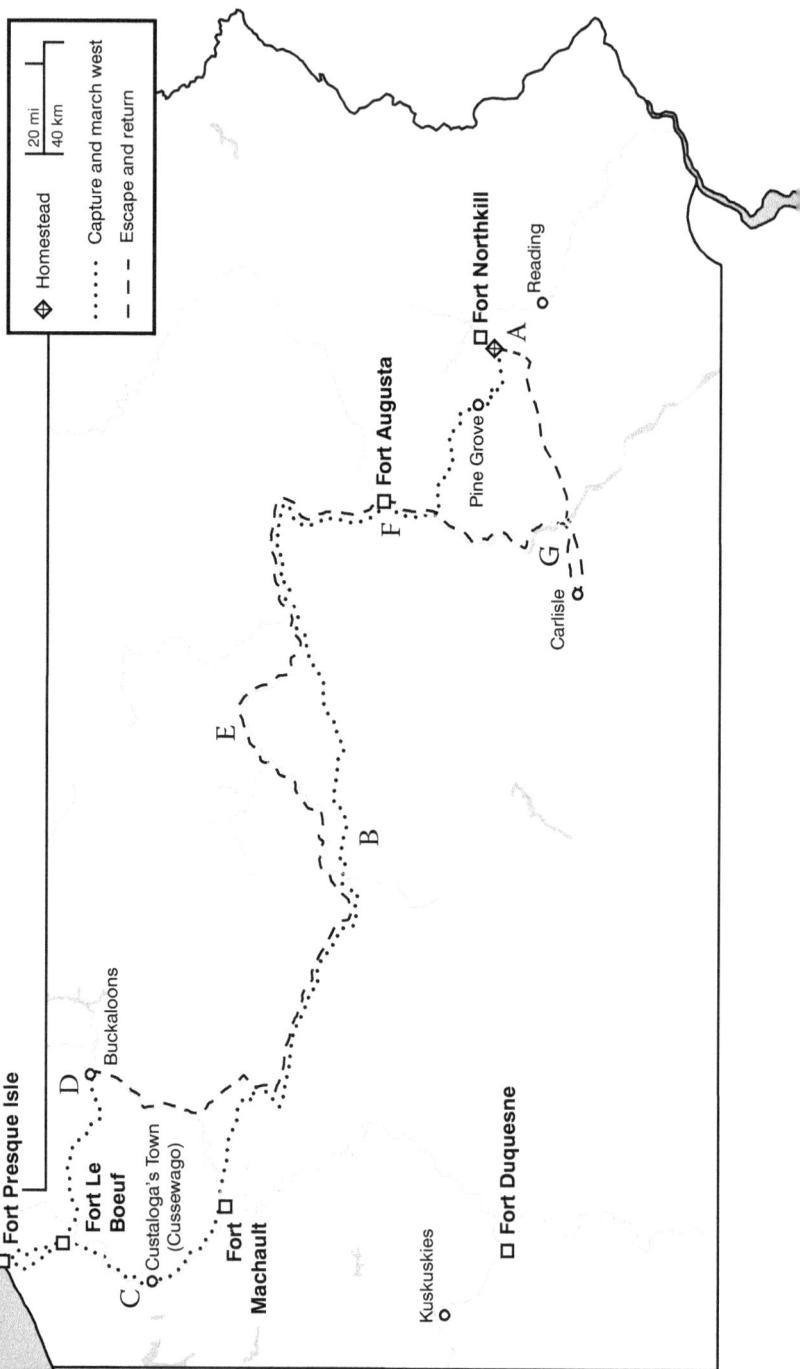

Guide to Map 4: Historical Locations

A—Jacob was captured in September 1757 and he returned home in June 1758.

B—The Indians and their captives walked westward for seventeen days.

C—"Custaloga's Town" (also Cussewago, or present-day Meadville). Custaloga's residence until 1763. Note: After the Indians reported to Fort Presque Isle, some of their captives were dispersed. Either Joseph, or his brother Christian, was taken back to Custaloga's Town to be adopted. He lived there six years.

D—Jacob was held at Buckaloons for about seven months (near present-day Irvine). He escaped in early May 1758.

E—Here Jacob made a raft.

F—Having floated on his raft for four days, Jacob was rescued May 24, 1758.

G—On his return journey, Jacob was taken with a unit of soldiers to Carlisle for a debriefing and then released to go home.

Letters above correspond to Map 4.

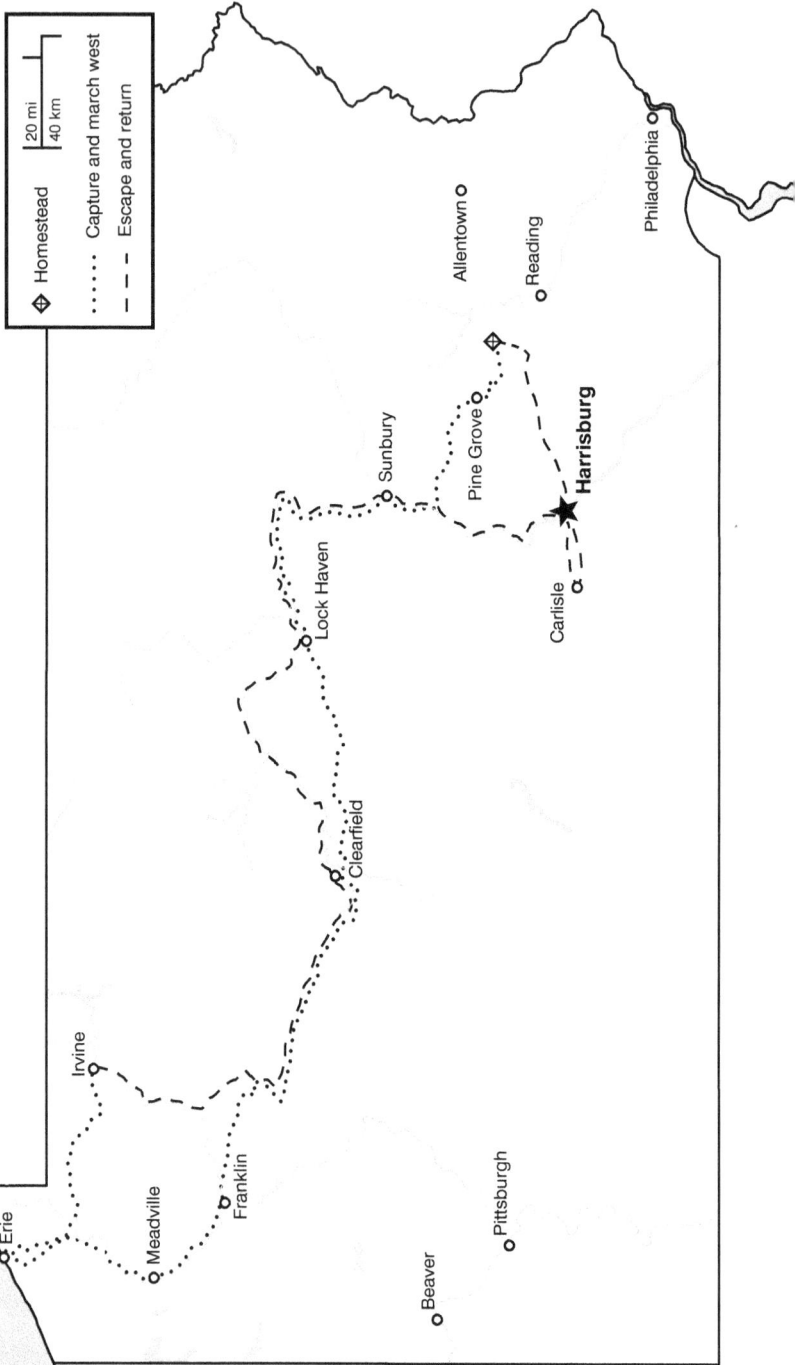

Map 5: Jacob's Journey in Relation to Present-Day Towns

Legend:
- ⊕ Homestead
- .... Capture and march west
- – – – Escape and return

20 mi
40 km

Towns: Allentown, Reading, Philadelphia, Sunbury, Pine Grove, Harrisburg, Carlisle, Lock Haven, Clearfield, Irvine, Meadville, Franklin, Erie, Beaver, Pittsburgh

Chronology of Jacob's Capture and Escape

This is a possible chronology for Jacob Hochstetler's capture, twenty-four-day trail walk, and escape. This chronology is based on Paul A. W. Wallace, *Indian Paths of Pennsylvania*, archival materials in Beth Hostetler Mark, *Our Flesh and Blood*, and a map drawn by Joseph Weaver.

Trail Walk: 1757

Day 1: September 20–21—Attack on the Jacob Hochstetler residence; Jacob and his sons were forced to march with the war party by an unknown path to present-day Rehrersburg. They then followed the Tulpehocken Path to camp near Pine Grove, between Blue Mountain and Second Mountain.

Day 2: September 22—Camped near Mahantango Creek, off Mahantango Mountain.

Day 3: September 23—Camped at Shamokin (present-day Sunbury); spied on Fort Augusta.

Day 4: September 24—Took the Great Shamokin Path and camped at Shickellamy's Town.

Day 5: September 25—Camped at Canaserage (present-day Muncy).

Day 6: September 26—Camped at French Margaret's Town or perhaps Queenashawakee.

Day 7: September 27—Camped at the Indian clearings.

Day 8: September 28—Traveled through the Great Island; camped at the fork of the Bald Eagle and Marsh Creeks.

Day 9: September 29—Camped at Snow Shoe Sleeping Place.

Day 10: September 30—Camped at Big Sand Spring Sleeping Place.

Day 11: October 1—Camped at Chinklamoose (present-day Clearfield).

Day 12: October 2—Took the Chinklamoose-Venango path to camp one-third of the way between Chinklamoose and Redbank Creek.

Day 13: October 3—Camped two-thirds of the way between Chinklamoose and Redbank Creek.

Day 14: October 4—Camped at the mouth of Sandy Lick Creek at Redbank Creek.

Day 15: October 5—Camped at Clugh's Riffle beside the Clarion River.

Day 16: October 6—Camped midway between Clugh's Riffle and Venango (present-day Franklin).

Day 17: October 7—Camped at Fort Machault at Venango (present-day Franklin).

Day 18: October 8—Took boats up French Creek north to camp at Custaloga's Town (twenty miles north of Venango).

Day 19: October 9—Camped at the confluence of French Creek and Muddy Creek.

Day 20: October 10—Camped at Fort Le Boef (present-day Waterford).

Day 21: October 11—Took Presque Isle Portage Path up to camp at Presque Isle (present-day Erie).

Day 22: October 12—Took Presque Isle Portage Path back down to Fort Le Boef; took the Brokenstraw Path east to camp at the fork of French Creek, just east of Fort Le Boef.

Day 23: October 13—Camped along Brokenstraw Creek not far east of junction with Hare Creek.

Day 24: October 14—Arrived at Buckaloons Village (present-day Irvine) late in the evening.

The total distance for this march (and short trip by boat) was approximately 430 miles. For a visual outline of these events, see Map 6. Numbers on the map correspond to the days of the trail walk.

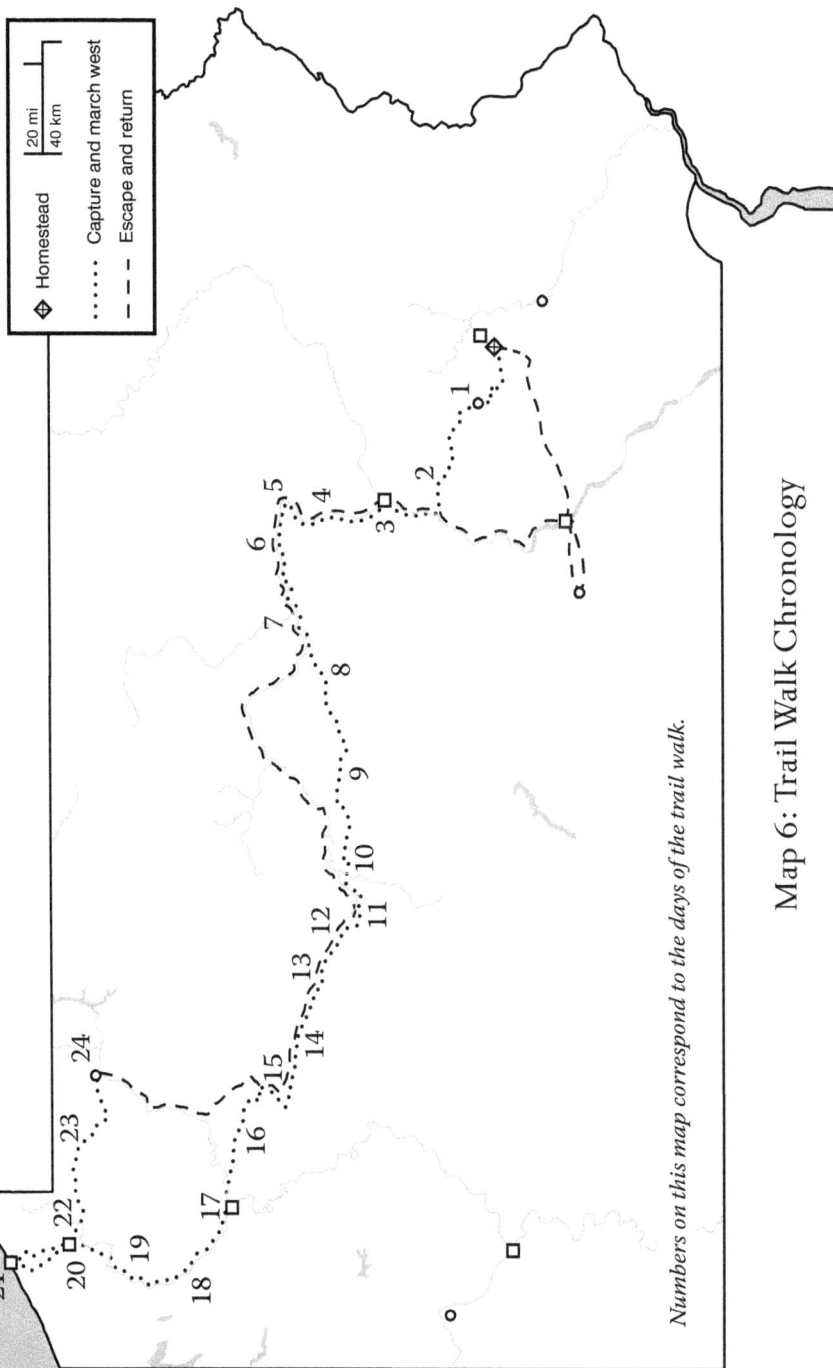

Scale:
20 mi
40 km

◆ Homestead
⋯⋯⋯ Capture and march west
‒ ‒ ‒ Escape and return

Map 6: Trail Walk Chronology

Numbers on this map correspond to the days of the trail walk.

Escape: 1758

May 9—Jacob escaped Camp Buckaloons and walked south and east until he came to the Goschooschink Path, and then followed it to the West Branch of the Susquehanna. He followed the river for several days to make sure he was on the right course.

May 19—Built a raft and started downriver on the West Branch of the Susquehanna.

May 24—Arrived at Camp Augusta at Shamokin; rode with Colonel Burd's troops along the Susquehanna River for several days.

May 28—Arrived at Colonel Bouquet's headquarters.

May 29—Took the Frankstown Path to Paxtang, and then the Allegheny Path to Weisers', and a local path to his home.

June 3—Arrived home.

Lancaster Longhouse

The story of Jacob Hochstetler's capture includes a number of scenes which take place in a Seneca longhouse. For several centuries preceding the adoption of individual homes, this was a common form of housing for the woodland Indians. In one of his journals describing a trip deep into Indian territory, Conrad Weiser describes his stay in an Iroquois longhouse.

The photograph below shows a recent full-size reproduction of a longhouse standing in a field in the former Pequea settlement next to the 1719 Hans Herr House, owned by the Lancaster Mennonite Historical Society. The Hans Herr House is the oldest house in Lancaster County and the oldest surviving Mennonite place of worship in the United States. For more than fifty years, the Lancaster Mennonite Historical Society and the 1719 Hans Herr House and Museum have told the story of Lancaster County, its settlers, and the role of the Mennonite community in the history of the region. Recently,

as part of their mission to represent the culture and context of Lancaster County's first European settlers, they began to collaborate with the First Nations Peoples' Circle Legacy Center in Lancaster and members of the local Native American community. That relationship led to the installation of a replica Native American longhouse to honor Pennsylvania's Native people and to tell a more complete Lancaster County story.

The longhouse harkens back to a time before white settlers came, when the Shenks Ferry, Conoy, Lenape, Mohawk, Nanticoke, Seneca, Shawnee, and Susquehannock had their homes in central Pennsylvania. Rather than being modeled after homes of specific tribes, the structure recreates features common to Eastern Woodland Indian construction between 1570 and 1770. The overall dimensions were based on a Susquehannock longhouse excavated in 1969 in Washington Boro, Lancaster County. The builders made slight concessions, such as using synthetic bark for the exterior, to improve its longevity, safety, and utility as an educational exhibit.

The longhouse is one of the few interactive outdoor exhibits of Native American life in Pennsylvania. It helps to instill awareness of the history of Pennsylvania before European settlement and Native influence on Lancaster County during the colonial period. It also introduces visitors to the contemporary Native American presence in Pennsylvania and supports the appreciation of ancient crafts practiced by local artisans as well as education about their lives, customs, and cultures. The interpreters at the Lancaster Longhouse help visitors understand the clash of cultures that occurred during the French and Indian War.

The 1719 Hans Herr House and Museum is located at 1849 Hans Herr Drive, Willow Street, PA 17584. More information is available at www.hansherr.org.

—Joel Horst Nofziger, director of communications,
Lancaster Mennonite Historical Society

Hochstetler Family Tree

This family tree of Jacob Hostetler, his first wife, their children, and their thirty-two known grandchildren is based on information compiled by Daniel E. Hochstetler. Other sources include *Harvey Hostetler's Descendants of Jacob Hochstetler (DJH), Descendants of Barbara Hochstedler and Christian Stutzman (DBH)* by the same author; and Hugh Francis Gingerich and Rachel W. Kreider's *Amish and Amish Mennonite Genealogies.*

Readers with Swiss-German Mennonite or Amish ancestors may be related to Jacob Hochstetler. To find out, readers should complete a five-generation family tree chart, to see if theirs connects with one of these families. Readers may also need to use Harvey Hostetler's *DJH* or *DBH* to make the connections. The numbers under the names will help to locate individuals in those books.

This family tree is incomplete and may contain some errors. For example, we don't know the names and birth dates of all the people in the genealogies. Uncertainty is indicated by question marks or brackets.

FAMILY TREE 1: [JACOB & [ELIZABETH] HOCHSTETLER

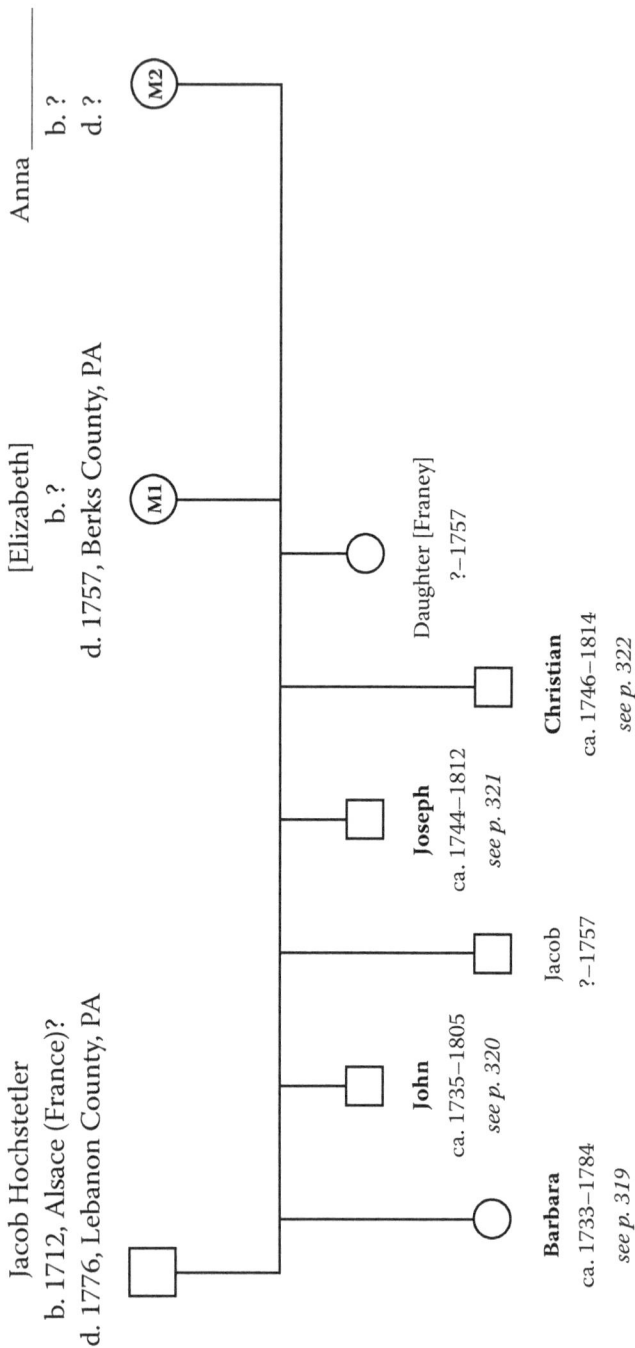

Jacob Hochstetler
b. 1712, Alsace (France)?
d. 1776, Lebanon County, PA

[Elizabeth]
b. ?
d. 1757, Berks County, PA

Anna
b. ?
d. ?

M1

M2

Barbara
ca. 1733–1784
see p. 319

John
ca. 1735–1805
see p. 320

Jacob
?–1757

Joseph
ca. 1744–1812
see p. 321

Christian
ca. 1746–1814
see p. 322

Daughter [Franey]
?–1757

FAMILY TREE 2: BARBARA HOCHSTETLER & CHRISTIAN STUTZMAN

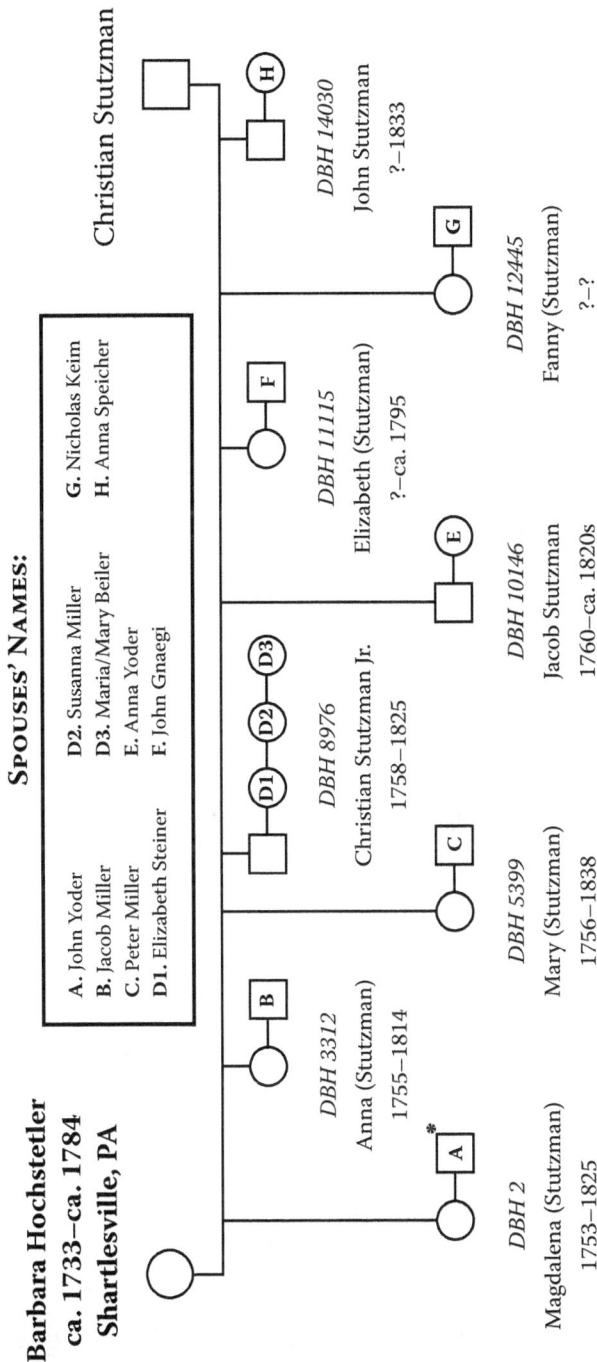

Barbara Hochstetler
ca. 1733–ca. 1784
Shartlesville, PA

Christian Stutzman

SPOUSES' NAMES:

A. John Yoder	D2. Susanna Miller	G. Nicholas Keim
B. Jacob Miller	D3. Maria/Mary Beiler	H. Anna Speicher
C. Peter Miller	E. Anna Yoder	
D1. Elizabeth Steiner	F. John Gnaegi	

DBH 2
Magdalena (Stutzman)
1753–1825

DBH 3312
Anna (Stutzman)
1755–1814

DBH 5399
Mary (Stutzman)
1756–1838

DBH 8976
Christian Stutzman Jr.
1758–1825

DBH 10146
Jacob Stutzman
1760–ca. 1820s

DBH 11115
Elizabeth (Stutzman)
?–ca. 1795

DBH 12445
Fanny (Stutzman)
?–?

DBH 14030
John Stutzman
?–1833

Spouses' full names can be found in the key above.

FAMILY TREE 3: JOHN HOCHSTETLER & CATHERINE HERTZLER

John Hochstetler
ca. 1735–1805
Summit Mills, PA

Catherine Hertzler

SPOUSES' NAMES:

A. Barbara Miller	D. UNKNOWN	G. Susanna Gieber	I2. Mary Eash
B1. Veronica Mast	E. Abraham Miller	H1. Barbara Schrock	J. Veronica Mast
B2. Elizabeth ———	F1. Elizabeth Schrock	H2. Sarah Yoder	
C. Jacob Yoder	F2. Mary Follmer	I1. Barbara Mast	

DJH 3
Jacob Hochstetler
ca. 1752–ca. 1813
(A)

DJH 1387
John Hochstetler Jr.
?–ca. 1813
(B1) (B2)
*

DJH 2798
Fanny (Hochstetler)
?–by 1827
(C)

DJH 3061
Catherine (Hochstetler)
?–?
(D)

DJH 3062
Anna/Aneli (Hochstetler)
?–?
(E)

DJH 4161
David Hochstetler
?–?
(F1) (F2)

DJH 4451
Joseph Hochstetler
1768–1823
(G)

DJH 4760
Henry Hochstetler
1773–1846
(H1) (H2)

DJH 5758
Daniel Hochstetler
?–1845
(I1) (I2)

DJH 6209
Jonathan Hochstetler
?–1823
(J)

*Spouses' full names can be found in the key above.

FAMILY TREE 4: JOSEPH HOCHSTETLER & ANNA BLANK

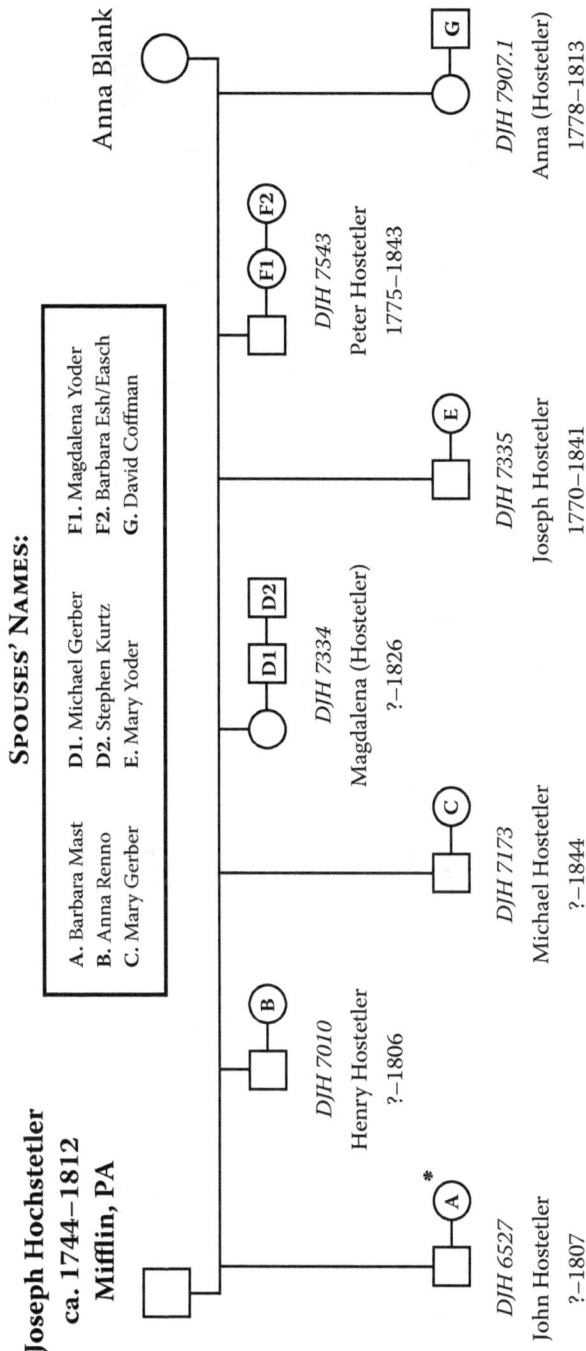

Joseph Hochstetler
ca. 1744–1812
Mifflin, PA

Anna Blank

SPOUSES' NAMES:

A. Barbara Mast	D1. Michael Gerber	F1. Magdalena Yoder
B. Anna Renno	D2. Stephen Kurtz	F2. Barbara Esh/Easch
C. Mary Gerber	E. Mary Yoder	G. David Coffman

DJH 6527
John Hostetler
?–1807

DJH 7010
Henry Hostetler
?–1806

DJH 7173
Michael Hostetler
?–1844

DJH 7334
Magdalena (Hostetler)
?–1826

DJH 7335
Joseph Hostetler
1770–1841

DJH 7543
Peter Hostetler
1775–1843

DJH 7907.1
Anna (Hostetler)
1778–1813

* Spouses' full names can be found in the key above.

FAMILY TREE 5: CHRISTIAN HOCHSTETLER & BARBARA RUPP

Christian Hochstetler
ca. 1746–1814
Dayton, OH

Barbara Rupp

SPOUSES' NAMES:

A1. Agnes Hardman	C. Christian Leatherman	E. Jacob Leatherman
A2. Nancy/Anna (Ashford) Munday	D. Jonas Snider	G1. Eulila Hoglan
B. Hannah Hardman	E. Elizabeth Hardman	G2. Elizabeth Wilcoxen

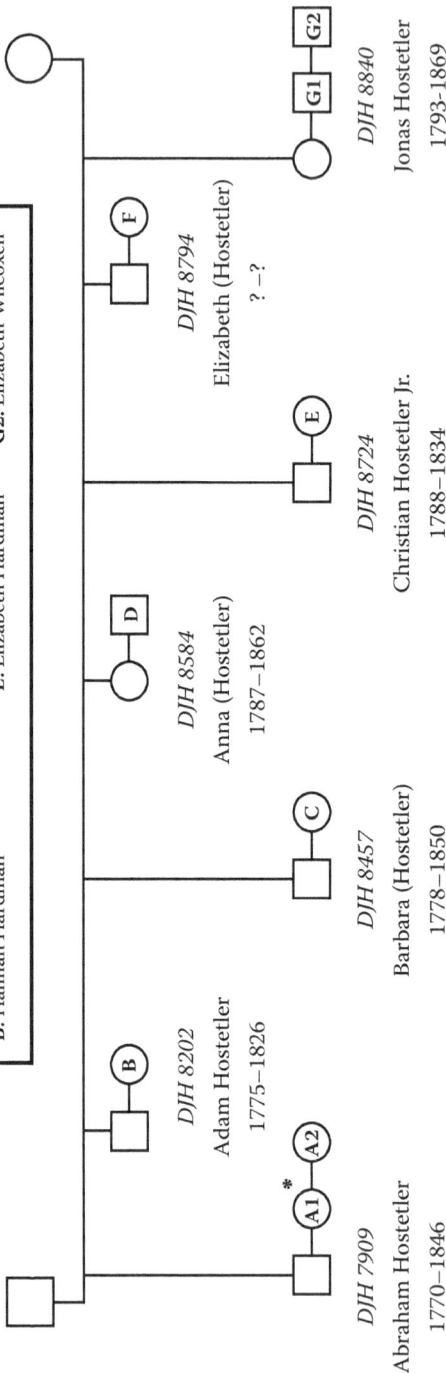

DJH 7909
Abraham Hostetler
1770–1846

DJH 8202
Adam Hostetler
1775–1826

DJH 8457
Barbara (Hostetler)
1778–1850

DJH 8584
Anna (Hostetler)
1787–1862

DJH 8724
Christian Hostetler Jr.
1788–1834

DJH 8794
Elizabeth (Hostetler)
? –?

DJH 8840
Jonas Hostetler
1793–1869

Spouses' full names can be found in the key above.

Historic
Anabaptist Beliefs

The seven articles of the Schleitheim Confession are considered a major source of distinctive Anabaptist beliefs. Widely believed to have been written by Michael Sattler, the seven articles of the confession were ratified by a gathering of Anabaptists in Switzerland in February 1527. The Dordrecht Confession, which is the primary confession of faith for Amish people today, largely reflects the beliefs contained within the Schleitheim Confession. Following are excerpts of the seven articles of the Schleitheim Confession.

The Seven Articles of the Schleitheim Confession
February 1527

The articles we have dealt with, and in which we have been united, are these: baptism, ban, the breaking of bread, separation from abomination, shepherds in the congregation, the sword, the oath.

I

Notice concerning baptism. Baptism shall be given to all those who have been taught repentance and the amendment of life and [who] believe truly that their sins are taken away through Christ, and to all those who desire to walk in the resurrection of Jesus Christ and be buried with Him in death, so that they might rise with Him; to all those who with such an understanding themselves desire and request it from us; hereby is excluded all infant baptism, the greatest and first abomination of the pope. For this you have the reasons and the testimony of the writings and the practice of the apostles. We wish simply yet resolutely and with assurance to hold to the same.

II

We have been united as follows concerning the ban. The ban shall be employed with all those who have given themselves over to the Lord, to walk after [Him] in His commandments; those who have been baptized into the one body of Christ, and let themselves be called brothers or sisters, and still somehow slip and fall into error and sin, being inadvertently overtaken. The same [shall] be warned twice privately and the third time be publicly admonished before the entire congregation according to the command of Christ (Matthew 18). But this shall be done according to the ordering of the Spirit of God before the breaking of bread so that we may all in one spirit and in one love break and eat from one bread and drink from one cup.

III

Concerning the breaking of bread, we have become one and agree thus: all those who desire to break the one bread in remembrance of the broken body of Christ and all those who wish to drink of one drink in remembrance of the shed blood of Christ, they must beforehand be united in the one body of Christ, that is the congregation of God, whose head is Christ, and that by baptism. For as Paul indicates, we cannot be partakers at the same time of the table of the Lord and the table of devils. Nor can we at the same time partake and drink of the cup of the Lord and the cup of devils. That is: all those who have fellowship with the dead works of darkness have no part in the light. Thus all those who follow the devil and the world, have no part with those who have been called out of the world unto God. All those who lie in evil have no part in the good.

So it shall and must be, that whoever does not share the calling of the one God to one faith, to one baptism, to one spirit, to one body together with all the children of God, may not be made one loaf together with them, as must be true if one wishes truly to break bread according to the command of Christ.

IV

We have been united concerning the separation that shall take place from the evil and the wickedness which the devil has planted in the world, simply in this; that we have no fellowship with them, and do not run with them in the confusion of their abominations. So it is; since all who have not entered into the obedience of faith and have not united themselves with God so that they will to do His will, are a great abomination before God, therefore nothing else can or really will grow or spring forth from them than abominable things. Now there is nothing else in the world and all creation than good or evil, believing and unbelieving, darkness and light, the world and those who are [come] out of the world, God's temple and idols. Christ and Belial, and none will have part with the other. [. . .]

Thereby shall also fall away from us the diabolical weapons of violence—such as sword, armor, and the like, and all of their use to protect friends or against enemies—by virtue of the word of Christ: "You shall not resist evil."

V

We have been united as follows concerning shepherds in the church of God. The shepherd in the church shall be a person according to the rule of Paul, fully and completely, who has a good report of those who are outside the faith. The office of such a person shall be to read and exhort and teach, warn, admonish, or ban in the congregation, and properly to preside among the sisters and brothers in prayer, and in the breaking of bread, and in all things to take care of the body of Christ, that it may be built up and developed, so that the name of God might be praised and honored through us, and the mouth of the mocker be stopped. He shall be supported, wherein he has need, by the congregation which has chosen him, so that he who serves the gospel can also live therefrom, as the Lord has ordered. But should a shepherd do something worthy of reprimand, nothing shall be done with him without the voice of two or three witnesses. If they sin they shall be publicly reprimanded, so that others might fear. [. . .]

VI

We have been united as follows concerning the sword. The sword is an ordering of God outside the perfection of Christ. It punishes and kills the wicked and guards and protects the good. In the law the sword is established over the wicked for punishment and for death and the secular rulers are established to wield the same.

But within the perfection of Christ only the ban is used for the admonition and exclusion of the one who has sinned, without the death of the flesh, simply the warning and the command to sin no more.

Now many, who do not understand Christ's will for us, will ask; whether a Christian may or should use the sword against the wicked for the protection and defense of the good, or for the sake of love.

The answer is unanimously revealed: Christ teaches and commands us to learn from Him, for He is meek and lowly of heart and thus we shall find rest for our souls. Now Christ says to the woman who was taken in adultery, not that she should be stoned according to the law of His Father (and yet He says, "What the Father commanded me, that I do") but with mercy and forgiveness and the warning to sin no more, says: "Go, sin no more." Exactly thus should we also proceed, according to the rule of the ban. Second, is asked concerning the sword: whether a Christian shall pass sentence in disputes and strife about worldly matters, such as the unbelievers have with one another. The answer: Christ did not wish to decide or pass judgment between brother and brother concerning inheritance, but refused to do so. So should we also do. [...]

VII

We have been united as follows concerning the oath. The oath is a confirmation among those who are quarreling or making promises. In the law it is commanded that it should be done only in the name of God, truthfully and not falsely. Christ, who teaches the perfection of the law, forbids His [followers] all swearing, whether true or false; neither by heaven nor by earth, neither by Jerusalem nor by our head; and that for the reason which He goes on to give: "For you cannot make one hair white or black." You see, thereby all swearing is forbidden. We cannot perform what is promised in the swearing, for we are not able to change the smallest part of ourselves.

An Early Twentieth-Century Account

The following is an excerpt from William F. Hochstetler, "Historical Introduction," *Descendants of Barbara Hochstedler and Christian Stutzman*, Harvey Hostetler, ed. (Berlin, OH: Gospel Bookstore, 1980; first published 1938; used here with permission). This excerpt is included as historical material that shaped the plot and some of the events portrayed in *Jacob's Choice*. While William Hochstetler researched some of this material in archives, much of it was passed down by oral tradition through several generations of Jacob Hochstetler's descendants. For many years, this material was the primary means by which Hochstetler descendants knew the story of their ancestor. Two corrections should be noted: on page 58, the essay asserts that Hochstetler was in captivity for three years. Later research (Mark, *Our Flesh and Blood*, pp. 16–18) gives evidence that he was held for only seven months. Also, on page 57, the essay suggests that Jacob was rescued at Fort Harris; more recent research shows this to have been Fort Augusta.

The reader should also bear in mind that the terms in this essay such as *savages* reflect the time period in which they were written. The material has been only lightly edited for the purpose of conforming to the publisher's style, along with a few minor corrections for the sake of clarity. Excerpted material is indicated by [. . .].

—*Ervin R. Stutzman*

Our Ancestor's New Home in America

Settlement of Pennsylvania. After William Penn had purchased, in 1682, from the British Crown the province of Pennsylvania, he went to the mainland of Europe to solicit settlers for his colony and found most ready acceptance from the Mennonites, whom he had previously visited as a representative of the Quakers. He visited Holland and the countries along the Rhine, where he found many Mennonites and Amish longing for a change. The inducements held out to them prompted many to emigrate to America, likewise many other Germans.

The first Swiss Amish to settle in America had years before emigrated to Alsace, Hessia, and the Palatinate. Some of the Jotters (Yoders), Oeschs, Gingerichs, Schlabachs, and others, when coming to America, spoke the Hessian dialect, but were originally Swiss. After about the year 1700, the Swiss Amish sometimes made their way direct to our country. Traveling at that time was tedious and crossing the ocean hazardous, and a journey from Switzerland to America required the greater part of a summer, an average ocean passage requiring about fifty days.

The registration law. So successful were the efforts made by the proprietors of Pennsylvania to secure settlers, and so ready were the oppressed Mennonites of Europe to avail themselves of the advantages offered in America, that many thousands found homes in the new land. The Germans, Swiss, and Palatinates came in such numbers that the provincial authorities became uneasy and finally, on September 27, 1727, passed an ordinance requiring the captains of ships to report the names and ages of their passengers, the place from which they came, and to state whether they came with intentions of becoming good citizens of the province. They also required the men over sixteen years of age to sign a declaration of allegiance to the province. This law makes it possible for many thousands of American citizens to know the name and date of arrival of their immigrant ancestors. [. . .]

Our Ancestor

Making a home. Our ancestor made a good selection of land, which lay east of the Northkill, a rapidly flowing creek which heads in the mountain and flows south into Tulpehoeken creek at Bernville, which in turn empties into the Schuylkill opposite Reading. Before the introduction of steam it furnished valuable water power. Shomo's Mill and an iron forge were near Hochstetler's home on the creek, probably built after the American Revolution. The buildings on both places are located some distance south of the state road leading from Harrisburg to Allentown, but the land extends across the road a considerable distance. The road probably at that time was not laid out. There seems to be no waste land to it, some being best adapted for pasture or permanent meadow, but the greater part is rolling and is a productive, tillable soil. It is about a mile west of the present village of Shartlesville, in Upper Bern Township, Berks County, Pennsylvania.

Perhaps not a tree or a bush had previously been removed. He selected a place for his buildings near a never-failing spring, which furnished fresh water for man and beast. In time the heavy timber was removed, the land cleared, and substantial buildings erected, all of which required hard labor and perseverance. Several acres of fruit trees were planted, and the usual hardships of frontier life gone through. But they enjoyed liberty to worship God as their conscience dictated.

At that time, reading material was scarce. The family library generally consisted of the Psalms, printed in a small volume, the New Testament, the Bible, with the German hymn book called the *Ausbund*, which at that time was in common use by the Amish. The book *Wandelmie Seele* was then found in nearly every home. There were in those days no public schools, and parents had their children taught in subscription schools or in the home. The education of the children was therefore limited. However, Jacob Hochstetler did not neglect the training of his children, for his son John was able to write a fair German hand, as appeared in a paper which the writer saw at Frederick Moyer's, bearing date February 1, 1755, which John witnessed. In due time John was married, his wife being Catherine Hertzler [. . .]. Good buildings were erected for him on the tract of land entered by the father, adjoining the old home farm on the south, also near a good spring, and so he was comfortably started near the old home.

First Amish church. The settlement in the Northkill became the home of what some claim as the first Amish church in America, an organization having been established as early as 1740. But the Yotiers and others settled in Oley Township much earlier and most likely had Amish among them, as there was an Amish congregation in that township. In 1742 there were enough of the nonresistant people living in this locality to petition the provincial assembly for exemption from the oath on being naturalized, a privilege which had already been granted the Quakers and Mennonites in Pennsylvania. Their request was granted. In 1749 Jacob Hertzler settled in this district and is claimed by some as being the first Amish bishop in America.

A second Amish settlement was made on the upper Conestoga, in Lancaster County, near the present Morgantown. This congregation is still in existence, while the one on the Northkill has long since disappeared.

Our ancestor was thus enabled to rear his family in the church of his faith. The congregation met for worship on the Sabbath at the homes of the members. In 1766 Richard and Thomas Penn donated to the Amish Mennonite congregation of Bern Township 20 acres of land for church, school, and graveyard purposes. The district extended along the south side of the Blue Ridge as far east as Hamburg. The settlement was not exclusively Amish, but good feeling prevailed throughout the neighborhood. The community grew steadily in population, and in 1752 it was deemed necessary to establish the county of Berks, made up of territory taken from Philadelphia, Lancaster, and Chester counties. On the first tax list of Bern Township, Berks County, appears the name of our ancestor, as well as the familiar Amish names of Jacob Hertzler, Christian Yoder, John Yoder, Christian Zoog, and Moritz Zoog. In the first list of Maxatawny Township appears the name John Hosteder in 1754, and John Hoffstatter in 1755, but does not appear later.

The French and Indian War

The old home, especially during the first years, was frequently visited by Indians, who gradually withdrew as the white settlers advanced. But as they had been fairly and honestly dealt with by the noble William Penn, they never molested the white settlers of the lower part of Pennsylvania after Penn settled there. A few depredations by white men committed against the Indians were promptly punished by the government. The Indians did the same thing with their bad men, so a general good feeling prevailed, until the beginning of the French and Indian War in 1754.

The Delawares. New Jersey and a large portion of Pennsylvania were inhabited by a powerful Indian tribe called Delawares—in their language, Lenni Lenape, signifying "Original People." They were divided into three sub-tribes: Unamis or "Turtle"; Unabachtgo, or "Turkey"; and the Minsi, also Muncie, or "Wolf Tribe." These tribes were again subdivided and received names from the localities where they lived. The Wolf tribe occupied the southeastern part of Pennsylvania including Berks County. The Moravians, originally from Austria and later from Herrenhut in Saxony, had commenced to do mission work among the Delawares at Oley ("hollow among hills"), also written Olink or Olo, which is east of the Schuylkill in Berks County. They had met with success and by their zeal and pious, Christian way of living, had gained the respect and confidence of the Red Man. Oley was for a long time the center of Moravian or Herrenhuter missions in different parts of the country, extending into the state of New York. During the terrible conflict between the English settlers of one part and the French and Indians of the other, the Indians at Oley remained peaceable and quiet, having adopted Christianity, and are scarcely mentioned in the old records.

Danger for border settlers. When the war broke out, it was evident that the settlers along the Blue Mountains, in Indian called Kittatiny, would be exposed to the tomahawk and scalping knife of the Indians. Very few settlers had ventured beyond the mountain. The government, with the help of nearby settlers, erected a number of forts along the mountain from the Delaware to the Susquehanna, with Fort Hunter on the Susquehanna, a few miles above the present Harrisburg, being the most westerly. Fort Manada on Manada Creek was next, being in Dauphin County. At Swatara Gap in Lebanon County was Fort Swatara; Fort Henry, or Dietrich Six, and Fort Northkill were in Berks County; Fort Franklin and Fort Lebanon in Schuylkill County; Fort Everest in Lehigh; and Fort Allen in Carbon County. Fort Harris was near the present Harrisburg, and farther north at the forks of the Susquehanna near Shamokin was Fort Augusta. These forts were constructed after the manner of those days to afford protection to the border settlers against the attack of the savage Indians. Whenever apprised in time the settlers took refuge in the forts, not one of which was taken or attacked during the war. The Indians carefully avoided them; sneaked through woods mostly in the nighttime and suddenly fell upon unsuspecting families; robbed and murdered them; and as suddenly disappeared before help could come from the forts. The country along the mountains seemed just suited to the Indian mode of warfare.

Cause of the war. The French who held Canada erected a number of forts on the lakes, also on the Ohio River, evidently intending to head off the English settlements westward. But to this the English would not submit; so hostilities were commenced, which at first proved disastrous to the English, the settlers in the colonies suffering the most. The French offered the Indians more for their land and better terms of trade than they received from the English and so induced them to join the French. The British sent an army elder, General Braddock, to capture Fort Duquesne, now Pittsburgh, which suffered a terrible defeat from the combined forces of the French and Indians on July 9, 1755. Emboldened by this victory, the Indians were led to believe that with the help of the French, they could drive all the English settlers from the country and regain their land. The Delaware Indians were not as warlike as the Iroquois, but having drawn northward and westward into their territory, were now in their power.

After the Indians had relinquished their claims to that part of the country inhabited by the Delawares and had sought habitations in other places, small roving bands frequently came through the settlements, begging their way, and caused no fear or terror among the people, who improved their farms and buildings, erected churches and schoolhouses, and enjoyed rural life in peace and tranquility. They had reason to believe that since they had very little to fear of the Indians while they were living almost among them, they certainly had nothing to fear from them when they had gone farther away. But emboldened by their success in routing the army under Braddock, the Indians began to move eastward in larger numbers toward the border settlements. The first murder in Berks County probably occurred in the month of November 1755. Under the date of November 19, 1755, Colonel Weiser wrote that he had just learned that the Indians for the first time had attacked settlers south of the Blue Mountains.

Fort Northkill. Fort Northkill was erected in February 1756, about two miles from Strausstown, to the north and east of that place, and about four miles from Shartlesville. This fort lay about midway between Fort Henry on the west and Fort Lebanon on the east, each about eleven miles away. The daily record of the officer in charge of this fort has been printed and covers the period between June 14, 1757, and August 31 of the same year. Under the date of October 4, 1757, Colonel Weiser speaks of enclosing the journal for the last month of his ensign at Fort Northkill.

The author of *Frontier Forts* assumes that this was the journal which ends with August 31 and which has been preserved. If such a journal was kept for the month of September 1757, it would doubtless mention the attack on the family of our ancestor. But if such a journal was kept, its whereabouts and contents are unknown. The author of *Frontier Forts* believes that the troops were withdrawn from Fort Northkill sometime in September, because early in October two lieutenants and forty soldiers were sent from Reading for the relief and protection of the settlers on the Northkill, which would not have been necessary had there been soldiers at the fort. At the same time Conrad Weiser urged strongly the return of his troops who had been taken from him to protect Fort Augusta, as the population had now left the country about that fort.

The account we have of the daily task of the soldiers of the fort is mainly the story of a constant scouting of soldiers through the woods between the forts and finding or seeing nothing of the enemy. The Indians often saw the soldiers doubtless and carefully kept out of sight. During August the farmers had requested the services of the soldiers for help in their harvest fields, and this help was given. The officers at the other forts were in constant need of more men and it may be that the Northkill force was taken to these other forts, and it may be that the military authorities were disposed to use their fighting forces to aid those who were ready to help themselves, as the Amish in the vicinity of Fort Northkill of course would not join in any fighting. A careful reading of the Northkill journal shows that the presence of the soldiers may have been a check to the depredations of the Indians, but did not entirely hinder their attacking the settlers living even within a short distance of the forts.

The summer of 1757. From the Northkill journal and other sources, we learn of attacks made by the Indians upon seven or eight families in the immediate neighborhood of our ancestor, upon families with whom he was personally acquainted. He would of course hear reports of murders of hundreds of others who lived at greater distances. A daughter of Andrew Wolbeck of Bern Township was captured by the Indians on November 2, 1756. The next day an attack was made on the family of Nicholas Long, near Fort Northkill, and two men were killed and Bernard Motz made captive. In this attack there were about twenty Indians, who were driven off by seven men from the fort, after seventeen farmers, doubtless noncombatants who had gone from the fort with the soldiers, had fled, leaving the seven to do the fighting. On the tenth of December of the same year, the house of Valentine Nigh or Neu, doubtless the fellow passenger and neighbor of our ancestor, was attacked, and one of his sons killed and another made prisoner. In the same month the wife of George Peter Gisinger, of Tulpehocken Township, was made captive, and the following April her husband was killed and scalped, and the same day a daughter of Balthazer Smith, of Bethel Township, was carried away captive. April 28th, 1757, John Adam Miller was killed at his home west of the mountain. The next murders were at the Meyers family, who resided about three miles from our ancestor. [. . .] The summer of 1757 was comparatively free from disturbance, though the Indians kept the settlers in a constant state of apprehension. None knew where the next blow would fall.

The Massacre

The attack. On the evening of September 19, 1757, that part of the country not having been disturbed since the Meyers murders in June, the young people of the neighborhood gathered at the home of Jacob Hochstetler to assist in paring and slicing apples for drying. At such gatherings it was the custom of the young folks after the work was done to have a social or frolic, sometimes continuing until late in the night. After the young folks departed the family retired; and just about the time they were sound asleep, the dog made an unusual noise, which awakened Jacob, the son, who opened the door to see what was wrong, when he received a gunshot wound in the leg. He realized in a moment that they were being attacked by Indians and managed to close and lock the door before the Indians could enter. In an instant all the family were on their feet. The Indians, eight or ten in number, were seen standing near the bake oven in consultation, evidently near daybreak, as there was no moon that night, the last full moon having occurred September 7. There being no light in the house, those inside could not be seen. There were several guns and plenty of ammunition at hand. Joseph and Christian picked up their guns to defend the family. Two or three could be shot and the guns reloaded before the Indians could gain an entrance, but their father, firmly believing in the doctrine of nonresistance, remaining faithful in the hour of sorest trial, could not give his consent. In vain they begged him; he told them it was not right to take the life of another even to save one's own. Joseph ever afterward claimed the family could have been saved had he given his consent, as they were both good, steady marksmen (their father also) and the Indians never stood fire unless under cover.

The house set afire. The Indians stood in consultation for a few minutes and then set the house on fire. The family consisted of six persons: the parents, Jacob Jr., Joseph, Christian, and a daughter, name not known. As the fire progressed, they sought refuge in the cellar, while the Indians stood guard around the house. When the fire had advanced so far as to burst through the floor, its advance was checked by sprinkling cider on the burning spots.

As daylight was now nearing, it was thought the enemy would not remain much longer and the family hoped to hold out until they departed. Meanwhile the disturbance attracted the attention of John, living on the adjoining farm. A few steps from his door he could see over to the old home, which being on fire, surrounded by the savages and all the family within, presented a shocking sight. The safety of his wife and child appealed to him. Hastening into his house, he took and concealed them in a thicket of brush in a flat place about eighty rods south of his house, and returned to see what could be done for those at the old home. There was no telling where the enemy might strike next; hence he prudently concealed his tracks, and on reaching a place where he could observe the old home, the Indians were just finishing their bloody work.

Family driven from the house. The family had kept quiet in their retreat, beating the fire back as best they could, and beheld the Indians leaving one after another. The stay in their retreat could scarcely be endured longer and, believing the enemy had all left, they proceeded to get out through a small window in the basement wall. As they emerged, a young warrior, Tom Lions, about eighteen years old, who had lingered behind gathering ripe peaches, observed them and gave the alarm.

The murders. The mother, being a fleshy woman, was with difficulty extricated; besides, the wounded Jacob had to be assisted. By the time the family were all out they were surrounded and were all easily captured except Joseph, who, being swift-footed like a deer, circled around, eluded them and ran up the hill, followed by two Indians who had thrown their guns away, determined to take him alive. He easily outran them and beholding them give up the chase and return to the burning building, he dropped down behind a log. It happened that one of the Indians observed him, but they hastened to the scene of carnage. The son Jacob and the daughter were tomahawked and scalped. But the mother, against whom they seemed to have a particular spite, was stabbed to the heart with a butcher knife and was scalped.

There is a tradition that years before hostilities broke out between the Delaware Indians and the white settlers, a party of Indians called at the Hochstetler home. Being in want, they begged subsistence but were refused and gruffly turned off by Mother Hochstetler. Some of them picked up a coal and drew a rude picture on the wall at the porch, which together with their grimaces forboded no good to the family, but seemed to indicate they were to take revenge. Some believe that but

for this unkindness the family would never have been molested; but when it is considered that over three hundred were
murdered in that section of the country alone, it is not likely
that our ancestors were singled out just for this unkindness.
The manner in which Mother Hochstetler was put to death,
however, shows that they had some special grievance against
her. The Indians at that time believed that to die under the
tomahawk or to be shot was the death of a warrior, and therefore an honorable death, but to die in some other violent way
was to them a dishonorable and disgraceful death; hence the
mother was killed in that way, they not having time to burn
her at the stake.

The prisoners. It is a tradition that when an Indian had
raised his tomahawk over the head of Christian, he looked up,
and as the Indian beheld his beautiful blue eyes, took a liking
to him and spared him. The disturbance had also attracted
the family of Jacob Kreutzer, residing to the west. They came
running through the woods to the edge of the meadow, but
on beholding what was going on they stopped, not being prepared to enter into a conflict with the savage foe.

The bloody work being finished, they took Jacob
Hochstetler and son Christian prisoners, left again in the direction they had started before, surrounding the place where
Joseph was concealed and easily captured him. Had he known,
he could easily have made his escape, but he feared he might
encounter Indians on ahead and so thought best to remain in
his hiding place. The barn and all out-buildings, including a
distillery, were destroyed by fire before the Indians left. The
father picked up some ripe peaches and advised his sons to
do likewise. He also advised them to submit gracefully to their
fate as far as possible. At this late date only a meager account
of all their experience can be given, and to understand such a
narrative, one ought to be familiar with the environments and
the manners and customs of the Indians at that time.

Impressions made by the massacre. The raid upon our
ancestor appears to have resulted also in several other deaths.

The reports show that a soldier, Philip Summer, was killed the same day and that Michael Spright (possibly Specht) and two children were made captive. The massacre made a profound impression. Under date of October 1, 1757, Colonel Weiser wrote to Governor Dewey, "Captain Oswald, upon hearing the distress the people about Northkill were in, sent immediately two lieutenants with forty private men to their assistance. I can not describe the consternation the people are in, in these parts."

Three days later he again wrote from Heidelberg, "It is now come so far that murder is committed almost every day; there never was such consternation among the people; they must now leave their houses again with their barns full of grain. Five children have been carried off last Friday; some days before a sick man [. . .] begged of the enemy to shoot him through his heart, to which the Indian answered, "I will," and did so. A girl that had hidden herself under a bedstead in the next room, heard all this; two more families were about that time destroyed." The last reference is made probably to the family of our ancestor and that of Michael Specht.

The massacre in the newspapers. In due time the news of the massacre reached the Philadelphia papers. *The Pennsylvania Journal* of October 6 had this: "From Reading we have advice that last Wednesday the enemy burnt the house of one Hochsteller and killed Hochsteller's wife and a young man, and himself and three children are missing." The other English paper in Philadelphia, the *Gazette*, about the same time had this: "We hear from Reading that on Thursday and Friday last some people were murdered in Bern Township by the Indians and others carried off."

The German paper in Philadelphia was *The Journal*, published by Christopher Sauer and issued twice a month. The issue of October 15, 1757, under a general heading, Philadelphia, October 7, has this: "In the same week the Indians came to Hoffstettler's place; the man called on his neighbors for help; meanwhile the Indians killed his wife and carried away his

children, and burnt the house and barn. One son escaped."
The same paper has the following from Tulpehocken, under
date of September 30: "I am sorry that I can not send you better news, as the Indians have again murdered many inhabitants beyond us. It is reported that there have been between
forty and fifty Indians not far from Nicholaus Langen's place.
The poor people beyond us will all be obliged to move away.
We stand in great fear. Yesterday we heard all day long of murder and death. No one however is ready to oppose the enemy."

The massacre in official reports. A little later Colonel
Weiser directed the officers at several forts to report to him
a list of those who had been killed or captured by the Indians
since the beginning of the war. [. . .] Extracts were printed in
the *Pennsylvania Magazine* for July 1908. Captain Jacob Orndt
reported among others, "Highstealer's wife and one child
killed and scalped; and three of his children taken captives
in September, 1757, in Bern Township." This list was made at
Fort Allen, and its author explains that he gives names and
dates as nearly correct as possible. Our family is mentioned
also in the report of Captain Jacob Morgan, who says that in
the district south of the mountains he is not absolutely cer-
tain of names and dates, but gives the best information he
can. Among those in Bern Township appears under date of
September 20, 1757, Jacob Houghstetler and family, five killed
and one wounded. The magazine account gives his name as
Houghstetter, and also fails to show that this report was made
by Captain Jacob Morgan.

The Captivity

Quite likely the prisoners' hands were tied and they made
to walk at a rapid pace, making for the Blue Mountains, which
are in sight of the Hochstetler home and about two miles dis-
tant on a straight line. There is a tradition that while crossing
the mountains they passed a clearing where a man named
Miller, an ancestor of the numerous Miller family now residing in Holmes County and adjoining parts of Tuscarawas

County, Ohio, was chopping. He was shot at and hit in the hand as he raised his ax; he fled and was not pursued. He may have belonged to the family of John Adam Miller, before mentioned as having been killed the previous April.

Indian abuses of prisoners. Prisoners were always subject to many abuses upon arriving at Indian villages; every old squaw or young Indian would hit them with switches and sometimes clubs and tomahawks. This was known to Hochstetler, who had saved some of the peaches from his home. He now with his sons approached the chief and those near him and presented them some peaches. This so pleased the chief that he immediately ordered the abuses stopped. It also saved them from going through what is called running the gauntlet, which was as follows: All Indians at the village or camp, both sexes, young and old, would stand in two rows facing each other, armed with switches, sticks, and sometimes tomahawks or other implements, and the unfortunate captive was made to pass through between the two columns, everyone striking and some endeavoring to impede their progress by throwing sand or dust into their eyes. Woe unto one that was slow in running; such a one was beaten unmercifully. At the end of the row stood the guardhouse, where the prisoner for the time was free; but some indeed never reached it.

A father's parting advice. Before the father and sons were separated, he gave them this parting advice in his Swiss dialect: "If you are taken so far away and be kept so long that you forget your German language, do not forget your names and the Lord's Prayer." A timely and good advice. Being separated, they rarely if ever saw each other. During their captivity they were made to conform to Indian customs and were gradually dressed in that style. Indians grow no beards and would not tolerate it among their captives, hence they pulled out Father Hochstetler's beard, also a part of the hair on the head, leaving a tuft or crown about four inches in diameter, which was braided and ornamented with feathers, etc. The pulling of the beard and hair on the head was done by taking a few hairs at a time and keeping on as if plucking a turkey until the job was completed to their notion. [. . .] The winter following was a severe one. Much snow fell in the mountains and lay a long time. The soldiers of Fort Northkill were withdrawn, until the snow was gone, and the severe winter increased the sufferings of the captives.

While in captivity our ancestor was never permitted to know where he was, except once when in Erie, Pennsylvania, and once in Detroit, Michigan. They moved frequently from one village or place to another. In some places but few Indians were together, while in other places large numbers gathered. [. . .]

The captivity of Jacob. We now resume the adventures of our ancestor Jacob. He never became reconciled to savage life but longed for his home, desolate as it was. He never gave up the idea of freeing himself in one way or other. He tried to conceal his desire and feelings, acting as if he were contented and reconciled, but Indians were hard to deceive and in spite of his pretenses, they never fully trusted him. The war had now lasted about six years since 1754 and during the last two years the English and Americans were mostly successful. Canada was taken from the French by the English but the Indians continued their raids. It was at a time when all the men or warriors had gone on a raid to the settlements that he concluded the time had come for him to escape, or die in the attempt.

His hunting trips. In the absence of the ablebodied men, Hochstetler was to provide for the families by procuring game. He was sent out daily to hunt, with orders to return at the close of the day if not sooner. He was given a gun, a few bullets, always counted, and a corresponding quantity of powder, with either a butcher knife or a tomahawk, but never both. On his return he was required to give an account of the ammunition used. If he did not bring home some game for every bullet used, he had to explain why he missed. He desired more than a daily outfit for his escape, so he prepared a dry place in a standing hollow tree, where he daily stored away a little powder and a few bullets, which together with the outfit of that day he considered sufficient to venture the undertaking. Of course, he never saved more than one bullet in any one day and was obliged to give an evasive or misleading account.

Where lay his home? But in what direction lay his home or the white settlements? And how far was he from the nearest settlements? These questions perplexed him. One day he noticed the old men explain something to the boys, using a stick with which they made rude marks in the ashes, which seemed to represent streams and mountains. He had acquired enough of the Indian language to understand they were making, in their way, a map of the country, showing the boys where their fathers had gone murdering. He dared not show that he understood what they meant, therefore passed to and fro apparently following his business, yet he managed to see them point to what seemed to represent a stream, which was called Susquehanna, another Allegheny, Monongahela, and mountains between these streams were named. It gave him a faint idea of his whereabouts and the course to pursue, as well as the distance to reach the settlements.

John Specht. There was another captive in the village, a German named John Specht whom he desired to take with him, and the evening before the planned escape he took him into his confidence. In so doing he had to be guarded, as the Indians were suspicious when they, or for that matter, any prisoners conversed in German with none of their people present who understood it.

The escape. The morning followed the night, and Jacob Hochstetler was sent out as usual with his outfit; this day the butcher knife was given him. Specht, having started under some pretense in another direction, met Jacob at an appointed place. The ammunition in the hollow tree was secured, and as much distance as possible put between them and the Indians they left behind, who were old men, squaws, and children, by whom there was not much danger of being pursued. The great danger to them lay in meeting hostile Indians who might return from their marauding, or might otherwise be scouring the woods.

A surprise. In the evening they concluded to encamp at a lonely place where there was an overhanging rock and where a fire could not be seen any distance. Imagine their surprise and embarrassment when on starting the fire, a lone Indian came to them. This unexpected visit put a damper on their spirits. Both parties tried to conceal their embarrassment. From the appearance of the Indian it was believed others were not far off, so Hochstetler immediately planned another escape. He advised Specht to gather wood for the fire, going a little farther every time he went for a stick and pretending he was looking for a larger stick, go out of sight and escape, while he picked up his gun, telling the Indian he would try to secure some game for supper. They were to meet farther up a little brook that ran close by. In talking to Specht he used the German, which was not understood by the Indian. Hochstetler waited at the upper end of the little run until dark, but Specht did not appear, so he returned and quietly approached their proposed camping place from above the rock. In doing this, he was obliged to use the utmost care to avoid being discovered. On reaching the edge of the rock, he carefully looked down. The fire had been suffered to go down and was not burning bright, no living being was seen, but by the glimmering fire he saw what he took to be fresh meat and blood.

Jacob flees alone. Believing the Indian had killed Specht and was watching for him, he stealthily crept back and renewed his flight, never stopping for the night's rest. He went on in the direction of his home, as ascertained before he started, and stopped for rest only when completely exhausted. He often concealed himself in the daytime and traveled at night. He crossed streams and mountains until he reached what he thought was one of the head branches of the Susquehanna, which he followed. Though he never knew whether he was at any time pursued, he always used due precaution, to prevent being followed in case an attempt was made, wading through water at times to prevent being tracked by dogs, and in daytime generally avoided paths. As he followed the stream it grew larger and prospects seemed to brighten, so he decided to float downstream on a raft, which first had to be built.

The raft. Having selected a place where fire could not be seen from a distance, he selected a dry fallen tree of proper thickness. Upon this he built some five or six fires at proper distances apart; the branches of the top and other small sticks were used, being laid crosswise on the log. In this way the thickest logs were burnt through. The process sometimes required several days. These were stirred and kept burning all night and by morning the trees were burnt through in as many places. The logs were dragged to the water, tied together with hickory withes or wild grapevines, and on this frail raft the journey was continued. After some distance the course of the stream turned to the right, and Jacob Hochstetler now believed he was on some other stream than the Susquehanna, probably the Ohio, which would take him away from home. He must have passed the present location of Pittston, Pennsylvania, about fifty miles to the north and a little to the east of his home. The river from this point follows a general southwestern direction till it reaches Duncannon, in Perry County, a few miles above Harrisburg, where it turns to the southeast. Fatigued and nearly starved, he tied his raft, and went on shore, about giving up in despair.

His dream. There is a tradition that he found a dead opossum full of maggots. He was so hungry that it tasted good and he ate till his hunger was appeased and then fell asleep, when his murdered wife appeared to him in a dream telling him to go on, that he was on the right way. When he awoke he took to his raft, determined never to leave it until he reached the white settlements. Thus he reached Fort Harris on the site of the present city of Harrisburg. He was too weak to stand, made efforts to be noticed, but failed to be observed until past the place. A little below the fort there was a place where the river was forded when low; here a man was watering a horse, who observed a strange object floating down stream; he went and reported. The commander at the fort with his spyglass discovered that there was a white man on a small raft and signaled to him, but all Jacob was able to do was to hold up his arm. He was accordingly rescued with a skiff. A woman, probably Mrs. Harris, prepared his first meals for him. He soon regained his strength and from here had no trouble in reaching his home. Before arriving at Fort Harris he must have passed two other forts, Fort Hunter about five miles above and Fort Augusta at the forks of the Susquehanna. From the latter the stream could not well be seen and Fort Hunter he may have passed in the nighttime. All in all, his adventures were hazardous, the escape marvelous, and his whole life replete with incidents worthy of being preserved to posterity.

The starting place. The place from whence our ancestor started when making his escape, and how long he was on the way on his perilous journey, is not known. It seems he must have been somewhere in northeastern Ohio, or in adjoining northwestern Pennsylvania, or possibly in the southwestern part of the state of New York, all that part being then inhabited by the Indians, and he probably was on the way from three to four weeks, as he could seldom travel fast and often could not go a direct course. The only game he secured during his flight was a wild duck, being afraid to shoot lest he be found out. Besides the wild duck, he subsisted on some crawfish, nuts, buds, and such edibles as could be obtained in the woods at that time of the year, which according to the manner in which the fire was to be built the first evening, must have been perhaps in September or October, after he was with the Indians about three years, about the time the French surrendered. It may also have been in the early spring, after the snows were gone, as the Indians often selected this season for their raids.

John Specht. The exact fate of John Specht was never known. He never reached the settlements, and when the lone

Indian later met the boys, Joseph and Christian, he made his boast that he had killed both their father and Specht, but his story was doubted by the boys. [...]

Councils at Easton. On the request of the Indians, a council was held with them at Easton, Pennsylvania, from October 8 to 26, 1758. This council was attended by Governor Dewey and others associated with him. A treaty of peace was agreed upon, and one of its conditions was that the Indians were to return all their prisoners and restore them to their friends, through General Johnson, who was to receive them. This treaty aroused the hopes of those who had lost relatives and friends, and we can easily believe that the sorrowing family and friends of our ancestor would rejoice at the news. Very few captives, however, were returned.

Speech of Governor Hamilton. After nearly three years, another council was held, August 3–12, 1761, at Easton, Pennsylvania, attended by Governor Hamilton. In his address to the Indians he reminded them of their former agreement about the captives and said, "Brethren, I am pleased to hear you sent to General Johnson, our flesh and blood who were prisoners among the Cayugas. We esteem it as the strongest proof of your friendship which you can possibly give us. You all agreed at the treaty held here three years ago that you would search all the towns and places in the Indian countries for them, and deliver them up to us, without leaving one behind, and if they had gone down your throats, you could heave them up again. I am sorry that but very few have yet been brought back, though I know there are a great many scattered up and down among the Indians. We cannot help thinking that you speak only from the lips and not from your hearts, whatever professions of regard you make for us, till this promise is performed, and we see our fathers, mothers, and children, who have been carried into captivity, restored to us. This promise was the condition on which the peace belt was exchanged between us." These vigorous words from the governor secured from the Indians another solemn promise that they would make every possible effort to restore all the captives that could be found among them. They agreed to bring them all to another council which was to be held the next summer at Lancaster.

Council at Lancaster. This solemn assurance of the Indians aroused a widespread interest and expectation among those who had lost relatives and friends. The council was to meet at Lancaster, and begin its session the twelfth day of August, 1762. Previous to this date, glowing reports came from the Indian country of the immense number of captives that were being brought and that would be turned over to their friends. We can easily imagine the eager interest with which our ancestor hastened to Lancaster, with the expectation of securing his long-lost sons.

A disappointment. But the council proved a deep disappointment. Instead of the hundreds of captives that had been promised and expected, there were about two dozen. But the Indians were very plausible in their excuses and apologies. They declared that the captives were unwilling to return, as they had become strongly attached to their Indian friends. The chiefs also claimed they found it hard to induce their people to drive from them the captives who were unwilling to return to the whites.

The council opened August 12. Our ancestor soon satisfied himself that his sons were not among the small number of restored captives, and he may have had tidings of them from Indians who were present. He was deeply disappointed, but would not give up to despair. But what could he do among the hundreds who were present looking for their captive friends? He was not accustomed to the transaction of business in a large public gathering such as this was. It is doubtful whether he could speak the English language, which was used by the men in charge of the council. But he was unwilling to leave the council till he had made at least some effort to secure the return of his sons. We can easily believe that he spent an anxious, troubled night, but in the morning he had decided what to do.

Jacob's petition. By the assistance of some friend, he prepared a petition which he presented to the Governor, who was very busy in the council, and who could ill spare the time for the needs of a humble individual like our ancestor. But the governor received the petition, which has been preserved. [...]

Petition of Jacob Hockstetter to Governor Hamilton, 1762

To the Honorable James Hamilton, Esq., Lieutenant Governor of Pennsylvania,

The Humble Petition of Jacob Hockstetler of Berks County, Humbly Sheweth:

That about five Years ago your Petitioner with 2 Children were taken Prisoners, & his wife & 2 other Children were killed by the Indians, that one of the said Children who is still Prisoner is named Joseph, is about 18 Years old, and Christian is about 16 Years & a half old. That his House & Improvements were totally ruined & destroyed. That your Petitioner understands that neither of his Children are brought down, but the Embassadour of King Xastateeloca, who has one of his Children is now here.

That your Petitioner most humbly prays your Honour to interpose in this Matter, that his Children may be restored to him, or that he may be put into such a Method as may be efiectual for that Purpose.

And your Petitioner will ever pray, &c.

Aug. 13, 1762.
his
Jacob X Hocksteter.
mark

Where was the petition written? This petition does not give the name of the place at which it was written, but it was evidently written at Lancaster, as seen in the words "now here," referring to the place where the Indian ambassador then was, at Lancaster with the governor holding the council. The words "brought down" would be appropriate at Lancaster, as used by one living in Berks County near the mountains, or it might refer to the higher regions to the north and west where the Indians lived. [. . .]

The ages of the sons. The age of the boys as given in the petition was 18 and 16½ years respectively, the petition dated August 13, 1762. The writer has reason to believe that the father had in mind their age at time of capture, that being the age given by my grandfather, who saw them both in later years, as well as their brother, John, who saw them being taken away. Besides, it is not likely that Joseph and Christian, if they were only 13 and 11½ years old, would pick up their guns to defend the family and beg their father to allow them to shoot, their parents belonging to the defenseless people. The writer has yet several palpable reasons why he thinks the father, in giving their age, had in mind the time of capture, but the reader can have his choice.

List of Sources

Anderson, Fred. *Crucible of War: The Seven Years' War and the Face of Empire in British North America, 1754–1766.* New York: Vintage Books, 2000.

Anderson, Niles, and Edward G. Williams. "The Venango Path as Thomas Hutchins Knew It. Introduction." *Western Pennsylvania Historical Magazine* 49, no. 1 (January 1966): 1–18.

———. "The Venango Path as Thomas Hutchins Knew It. Part II. From Venango to Presqu' Isle." *Western Pennsylvania Historical Magazine* 49, no. 2 (April 1966): [141]–154.

Angevine, Erma Miller. "Some Early Hostetler Documents with Comments, Part One." *Hochstetler/Hostetler/Hochstedler Family Newsletter* VII, no. 4 (December 1993): 6–7.

———. "Some Early Hostetler Documents with Comments, Part Two." *H/H/H Family Newsletter* VIII, no. 1 (March 1994): 4–5.

———. "Some Early Hostetler Documents with Comments, Part Three (Concluded)." *H/H/H Family Newsletter* VIII, no. 2 (June 1994): 3–4.

Axtell, James. "The White Indians of Colonial America." *William and Mary Quarterly, Third Series* 32, no. 1 (January 1975).

Bartram, John, and Peter Kalm. *Observations on the Inhabitants, Climate, Soil, Rivers, Productions, Animals, and Other Matters Worthy of Notice Made By Mr. John Bartram, in His Travels From Pensilvania to Onondago, Oswego and the Lake Ontario, in Canada.* London: J. Whiston & B. White, 1751.

Beachy, Leroy. *Unser Leit: The Story of the Amish.* 2 vols. Millersburg, OH: Goodly Heritage Books, 2011.

Bender, Wilbur J. *Nonresistance in Colonial Pennsylvania.* 4th printing. Harrisonburg, VA: Eastern Mennonite Publications, 1985.

Bradley, John. *Conrad Weiser Homestead.* Series: Pennsylvania Trail of History Guide. Mechanicsburg, PA: Stackpole Books, 2001.

Brumbaugh, G. Edwin. "Colonial Architecture of Pennsylvania Germans." Address before the forty-first annual meeting of the Pennsylvania German Society at Reading, October 23, 1931. Breiningsville, PA: Pennsylvania German Society, 1933.

Byler, John M. *Alte Schreibens: Amish Documents and Record Series.* Sugarcreek, OH: Schlabach Printers, 2008.

———. *Trials of the Hochstetler Family.* Second printing. Self-published, 2008.

Davis, Kenneth C. *America's Hidden History: Untold Tales of the First Pilgrims, Fighting Women, and Forgotten Founders Who Shaped a Nation.* New York: Smithsonian Books, 2008.

Donehoo, George P. *Indian Villages and Place Names in Pennsylvania.* Baltimore: Gateway Press, 1995. First published in 1928.

Dowd, Gregory Evans. *War under Heaven: Pontiac, The Indian Nations and the British Empire.* Baltimore: Johns Hopkins University Press, 2002.

Drimmer, Frederick. *Captured by the Indians: 15 Firsthand Accounts, 1750–1870.* Toronto: General Publishing Company, 1961.

Durnbaugh, Donald F. "Christopher Sauer and his Germantown Press." *Der Reggenbote: Quarterly of the Pennsylvania German Society* 4, no. 2 (June 1970): 3–16.

"Early Amish Land Grants in Berks County, Pennsylvania." Papers. Pequea Bruderschaft Library, Gordonville, PA.

Eshleman, Henry Frank. *Lancaster County Indians: Annals of the Susquehannocks and Other Indian Tribes of the Susquehanna Territory from about the Year 1500 to 1763, the Date of Their Extinction* . . . . Lancaster, PA: Express Print Co., 1909.

Feest, Christian F. *Indians of Northeastern North America.* Leiden, Netherlands: E.J. Brill, 1986.

Fogleman, Aaron Spencer. *Hopeful Journeys: German Immigration, Settlement, and Political Culture in Colonial America, 1717–1775.* Philadelphia: University of Pennsylvania Press, 1996.

Gilbert, Benjamin. *A Narrative of the Captivity and Sufferings of Benjamin Gilbert and His Family, Who Were Taken by the Indians in the Spring of 1780.* Philadelphia: John Richards, 1848. Available on Google Books.

Gilbert, Russell W. "The Almanac in Pennsylvania German Homes." *Morning Call* (Allentown, PA), January 8, 1944.

———. "An Old Recipe for the Making of Ink." *Morning Call* (Allentown, PA), February 23, 1946.

Gill, Sam D. *Native American Religions: An Introduction.* Belmont, CA: Wadsworth Publishing Company, 1982.

———. *Native American Traditions: Sources and Interpretations.* Belmont, CA: Wadsworth Publishing Company, 1983.

Gingerich, Hugh Francis, and Rachel W. Kreider. *Amish and Amish Mennonite Genealogies*, rev. ed. Gordonville, PA: Pequea Bruderschaft Library; Morgantown, PA: Masthof Press, 2007.

Glick, Ervie Lowell. *From the Judith to the Round Barn: A Peter Glück Family History.* Harrisonburg, VA: E. L. Glick, 2009.

Gross, Leonard, trans. and ed. *Prayer Book for Earnest Christians (Die ernsthaft Christenpflicht).* Scottdale, PA: Herald Press, 1997.

Grumet, Robert S. *The Lenapes.* New York: Chelsea House Publishers, 1989.

Heckewelder, John Gottlieb Ernestus. *History, Manners, and Customs of the Indian Nations Who Once Inhabited Pennsylvania and the Neighboring States.* Memoirs of the Historical Society of Pennsylvania, XII. Philadelphia: Publication Fund of the Historical Society of Pennsylvania, 1881.

Heeter, Ken J. *Index to "Bishop Jacob Hertzler and His Family" by Paul V. Hostetler 1976.* Bel Air, MD: K. J. Heeter, 1986.

Hertzler, John. *A Brief Biographic Memorial of Jacob Hertzler: And a Complete Genealogical Family Register of His Lineal Descendants and Those Related by Inter-marriage, from 1730 to 1883, Chronologically Arranged . . . Also An Appendix of, The Christian Zug Family.* Port Royal, PA: J. Hertzler, 1885.

History of Venango County, Pennsylvania . . . Chicago, IL: Brown, Runk and Co., Publishers, 1890.

Hochstättler, Erwin. 1989. "Traces of Jacob Hochstetler's Relatives in Europe." *H/H/H Newsletter* III, no. 3 (December 1989): 3–5.

———. "Anabaptist Preacher Jacob Hochstetler at Ste. Marie-aux-Mines (Markirch) in 1720." *H/H/H Family Newsletter* XX, no. 3 (June 2006): 5–6.

Hochstetler, Daniel E. "Hochstedler Document Raises New Questions." *H/H/H Family Newsletter* IV, no. 4 (December 1990): 4, 7–8.

———. "Origin of H/H/H Family and Name." *H/H/H Family Newsletter* VI, no. 1 (March 1992): 6–7.

———. "Stutzman Farms in Berks County." *H/H/H Family Newsletter* X, no. 2 (June 1996): 7–8.

———. "Jacob Hochstetler's Last Farm." *H/H/H Family Newsletter* X, no. 4 (December 1996): 4–5, 8.

———. "Jacob Hochstedler's 1765 Farm." *H/H/H Family Newsletter* XI, no. 3 (September 1997): 1, 3, 6.

———. "Unsolved Mysteries Concerning Jacob Hostetler." *H/H/H Family Newsletter* XV, no. 1 (March 2001): 4–6, 8.

———. "'Corrections' Concerning Jacob Hochstetler." *H/H/H Family Newsletter* XV, no. 3 (September 1997): 3–7.

———. "A Dozen Ways to Spell Our Name, Part 1." *H/H/H Family Newsletter* XVI, no. 2 (June 2001): 6–7.

———. "A Dozen Ways to Spell Our Name, Part 2." *H/H/H Family Newsletter* XVI, no. 3 (September 2002): 9.

———. "A Dozen Ways to Spell Our Name, Part 3." *H/H/H Family Newsletter* XVI, no. 4 (December 2002): 8–9.

———. "A Dozen Ways to Spell Our Name, Part 4." *H/H/H Family Newsletter* XVII, no. 1 (March 2002): 6–7.

———. "A Dozen Ways to Spell Our Name, Part 5." *H/H/H Family Newsletter* XVII, no. 3 (September 2003): 8.

———. "A Dozen Ways to Spell Our Name, Part 6." *H/H/H Family Newsletter* XVII, no. 4 (September 2003): 7, 10.

———. "A Dozen Ways to Spell Our Name, Part 7." *H/H/H Family Newsletter* XVIII, no. 1 (March 2004): 3–6.

———. "A Dozen Ways to Spell Our Name, Part 8." *H/H/H Family Newsletter* XVIII, no. 2 (June 2004): 9–10.

———. "A Short History of the Jacob Hochstetler Family." *H/H/H Family Newsletter* XX, no. 4 (December 2006): 7.

———. "Service of Commemoration of the 250th Anniversary of the Massacre of Members of the Hostetler Family." *H/H/H Family Newsletter* XXI, no. 4 (December 2007): 1, 3.

———. "The Jacob Hochstetler Spring." *H/H/H Family Newsletter* XXV, no. 3 (September 2011): 9–10.

———. "From Bake Oven to Memorial Monument." *H/H/H Family Newsletter* XXV, no. 4 (December 2011): 1, 4–5.

Hollenbach, Raymond E. "Something About Nails." *Morning Call* (Allentown, PA), December 29, 1945.

Hostetler, Harvey. *Descendants of Jacob Hochstetler*. Historical Introduction by William F. Hochstetler. Berlin, OH: Gospel Bookstore, 1977. First published 1912.

———. *Descendants of Barbara Hochstedler and Christian Stutzman*. Historical Introduction by William Hochstetler. Berlin, OH: Gospel Bookstore, 1980. First published 1938.

Hostetler, Jonathan J. "Jacob Hochstetler: Immigrant of 1738." *H/H/H Family Newsletter* IV, no. 3 (September 1990): 1, 3.

Hostetler, Paul V. "John Hochstetler, Sr., Son of the Immigrant." *H/H/H Family Newsletter* XII, no. 2 (April 1988): 4.

Hultkrantz, Åke, Joseph Epes Brown, N. Scott Momaday, Sam D. Gill, Emory Sekaquaptewa, W. Richard Comstock, and Barre Toelken. *Seeing with a Native Eye: Essays on Native American Religion.* Edited by Walter Holden Capps and Ernst F. Tonsing. New York: Harper & Row, 1976.

Jacobs, Wilbur R. *Diplomacy and Indian Gifts: Anglo-French Rivalry Along the Ohio and Northwest Frontiers, 1748–1763.* Originally published Stanford University Press, 1950. Lewisburg, PA: Wennawoods Publishing, 2001.

Juhnke, James C. "How Our Ancestors Made Peace with Death." *Mennonite World Review,* October 15, 2012, 9.

King, Amos. "Gordonville, PA, Ridge Rd." *Die Botschaft,* December 23, 1992, 25.

Kraft, Herbert C. *The Lenape: Archeology, History and Ethnography.* Trenton: New Jersey Historical Commission, 1986.

———. *The Lenape or Delaware Indians: The Original People of New Jersey.* South Orange, NJ: Seton Hall University Museum, 1996.

Landis, Ira D. "Mennonite Agriculture in Colonial Lancaster County, Pennsylvania." *Mennonite Quarterly Review* 19, no. 4 (1945): 254–72.

Leach, Douglas Edward. *The Northern Colonial Frontier, 1607–1763.* Histories of the American Frontier. Ray Allen Billington, series ed. New York: Holt, Rinehart and Winston, 1966.

Luthy, David. "Two Waves of Amish Migration to America." *Family Life* (March 1988), 20–24.

———. "Immigrant Jacob Hochstetler's European *Ausbund.*" *Mennonite Family History* (April 1988): 62–64.

MacMaster, Richard K., Samuel L. Horst, and Robert F. Ulle. *Conscience in Crisis: Mennonites and Other Peace Churches in America, 1739–1789: Interpretation and Documents*. Scottdale, PA: Herald Press, 1979.

Mark, Beth Hostetler. "Compilers' Comments: Our Flesh and Blood." *H/H/H Family Newsletter* XVII, no. 4 (December 2003): 3–4.

———, ed. *Our Flesh and Blood: A Documentary History of The Jacob Hochstetler Family During the French and Indian War Period, 1757–1765*. 3rd ed. Elkhart, IN: Jacob Hochstetler Family Association, 2003.

———. "White Indians: One Voice for Native American History." Unpublished manuscript, May 4, 1992.

Mast, J. Lemar, and Lois Ann Mast. *As Long as the Wood Grows and Water Flows: A History of the Conestoga Mennonite Church*. Morgantown, PA: Tursack Printing, 1982.

Mast, Lois Ann. *The Peter Leibundgutt Journal*. Elverson, PA: Masthof Press, 1991.

McGrath, William R. *Christian Discipline: How and Why the Anabaptists Made Church Standards: Being a Collection and Translation of Anabaptist and Amish-Mennonite Church Disciplines from 1527, 1568, 1607, 1630, 1668, 1688, 1779, 1809, 1837, 1865, and 1964, with Historical Explanations and Notes*. Millersburg, OH: Amish Mennonite Publications, n.d. First published as *Christlicher Ordnung or Christian Discipline*. Aylmer, ON: Pathway Publishers, 1966.

———. *Contentment: The Life and Times of Jacob Hertzler, Pioneer Amish Bishop, 1703–1786*. Minerva, OH: Christian Printing Mission, 1984.

McVey, John Jos. *Gottlieb Mittleberger's Journey to Pennsylvania in the Year 1750 and Return to Germany in the Year 1754*. Philadelphia: University of Pennsylvania, 1898 edition.

Merrell, James H. *Into the American Woods: Negotiators on the Pennsylvania Frontier.* New York: W.W. Norton and Company, 1999.

Merritt, Jane T. *At the Crossroads: Indians and Empires on a Mid-Atlantic Frontier, 1700–1763.* Chapel Hill: University of North Carolina Press and Williamsburg, VA: Omohundro Institute of Early American History and Culture, 2011.

Michener, Carolee K., and Michael J. O'Malley III. "Venango County Indians, Oil, Ghost Town." *Pennsylvania Heritage* 10, (Spring 1984): 32–37.

Miller, Ivan I. "The Tom Lion Legend." *H/H/H Family Newsletter* XI, no. 2 (June 1997): 1, 6–7.

Miller, J. Virgil. "Amish-Mennonites in Northern Alsace and the Palatinate in the Eighteenth Century and their Connection with Immigrants to Pennsylvania." *Mennonite Quarterly Review* 50, no. 4 (October 1976): 272–80.

———. "From an Indian Perspective." *H/H/H Family Newsletter* VI, no. 3 (September 1992): 3–4.

———. "Jacob Hochstetler Arrived in 1738." *H/H/H Family Newsletter* I, no. 2 (December 1998): 6.

———. "Who Was Jacob Hochstetler's Wife?" *H/H/H Family Newsletter* XIV, no. 4 (December 2000): 5–6.

———. *Both Sides of the Ocean: Amish-Mennonites from Switzerland to America.* Morgantown, PA: Masthof Press, 2002.

———. "The Northkill Amish Settlement." *H/H/H Family Newsletter* XXII, no. 4 (December 2008): 6–7.

———. "The Tulpehocken Settlement." *H/H/H Family Newsletter* XXIII, no. 2 (June 2009): 1–2.

Minutes of the Provincial Council of Pennsylvania, From the Organization to the Termination of the Proprietary Government. Published by the State. Vol. VIII. Containing the Proceedings of Council from January 13, 1757, to October 4, 1762, Both Dates Included. Harrisburg, PA: Theo. Penn and Co., 1852.

Myers, Albert Cook, ed. *William Penn's Own Account of the Lenni Lenapi or Delaware Indians.* Moorestown, NJ: Middle Atlantic Press, 1970.

Namias, June. *White Captives: Gender and Ethnicity on the American Frontier.* Chapel Hill: University of North Carolina Press, 1993.

Neff, Larry M., and Frederick S. Weiser, trans. and ed. "Conrad Weiser's Account Book." In *Sources and Documents of the Pennsylvania Germans VI*, Frederick Weiser, series editor. Breiningsville, PA: Pennsylvania German Society, 1981.

Olmstead, Earl P. *David Zeisberger: A Life among the Indians.* Kent, OH: Kent State University Press, 1997.

Pemberton, James. "Journal of James Pemberton at the Lancaster Treaty, 1762," in *Indian Treaties Printed by Benjamin Franklin.* Philadelphia: Historical Society of Pennsylvania, 1762/1938. http://bit.ly/1ebGiKs.

Post, Christian Frederick. "Journey on the Forbidden Path: Chronicles of a Diplomatic Mission to the Allegheny Country, March-September 1760." Edited by Robert S. Grumet. *Transactions of the American Philosophical Society*, New Series 89, no. 2 (1999): i–v, vii, ix–x, 1–156.

Richards, Henry Melchior Muhlenberg. "Pennsylvania: The German Influence on Its Settlement and Development. A Narrative and Critical History. Part IV." *The Pennsylvania-German in the French and Indian War.* Proceedings of The Pennsylvania-German Society. October 25, 1904.

Richter, Daniel K. *Facing East from Indian Country: A Native History of Early America.* Cambridge, MA: Harvard University Press, 2001.

Rivinus, Willis M. *William Penn and the Lenape Indians.* New Hope, PA: Self-published, 1995.

Schabalie, John Philip. *The Wandering Soul, or Conversations of the Wandering Soul with Adam, Noah, and Simon Cleophas, Containing A Brief Summary of Leading Historical Facts from the Creation of the World to A.D. 109. Together with a Full Account of the Destruction of Jerusalem. Translated Originally from the Hollandish Into German and from the German into English.* Baltic, OH: Raber Book Store, 2005. Original Dutch edition 1635.

Schnure, William Marion, comp. *Selinsgrove, Penna. Chronology, Volume One, 1700–1850.* Middleburg, PA: Middleburg Post, 1918.

Schoenfeld, Max. *Fort de la Presqu'ile and The French Penetration into the Upper Ohio Country, 1753–1759.* Erie, PA: Erie County Historical Society, 1979. Reprinted 1997.

Silver, Peter. *Our Savage Neighbors: How Indian War Transformed Early America.* New York: W. W. Norton and Company, 2008.

Sipe, C. Hale. *The Indian Wars of Pennsylvania: An Account of the Indian Events, in Pennsylvania, of the French and Indian War, Pontiac's War, Lord Dunmore's War, the Revolutionary War and the Indian Uprising from 1789–1795,* 2nd ed. Lewisburg, PA: Wennawoods Publishing, 1999. Originally published Butler, PA: 1931.

Slabaugh, John M. "The Value and Use of Pennsylvania's Connected Warrantee Maps." *Mennonite Family History* (January 1987): 20–22.

Stein, Stephen J. *Communities of Dissent: A History of Alternative Religions in America.* New York: Oxford University Press, 2003.

Stoltzfus, Grant M. *History of the First Amish Mennonite Communities in America.* Harrisonburg, VA: Research Department of Eastern Mennonite College, 1958.

Todish, Tim J. *The Narrative Art of Robert Griffing: Volume II, The Journey Continues.* New York: Paramount Press, Inc., 2007.

Tooker, Elisabeth, ed. *Native North American Spirituality of the Eastern Woodlands: Sacred Myths, Dreams, Visions, Speeches, Healing Formulas, Rituals, and Ceremonials.* Classics of Western Spirituality series. New York: Paulist Press, 1979.

Verrill, A. Hyatt. *Foods America Gave the World.* Boston: L. C. Page and Company, 1937.

Volwiler, A. T. "George Croghan and the Westward Movement, 1741–1782 (continued)." *Pennsylvania Magazine of History and Biography* 47, no. 1 (1923): 28–57.

Wallace, Paul A. W. *Indian Paths of Pennsylvania.* Harrisburg, PA: Pennsylvania Historical and Museum Commission, 2005.

———. *Indians in Pennsylvania.* Harrisburg, PA: Pennsylvania Historical and Museum Commission, 1989.

Ward, Matthew C. "Redeeming the Captives: Pennsylvania Captives among the Ohio Indians, 1755–1765." *Pennsylvania Magazine of History and Biography* 125, no. 3 (July 2001): 161–89.

Weidensaul, Scott. *The First Frontier: The Forgotten History of Struggle, Savagery, and Endurance in Early America.* Boston: Houghton Mifflin Harcourt, 2012.

Wenning, Scott Hayes. *Handbook of the Delaware Indian Language: The Oral Tradition of a Native People.* Lewisburg, PA: Wennawoods Publishing, 2000.

Weslager, C. A. *The Delaware Indians: A History.* New Brunswick, NJ: Rutgers University Press, 1972.

Wood, Jerome H. *Conestoga Crossroads: The Rise of Lancaster, Pennsylvania, 1730–1789.* PhD diss., Brown University, 1969.

Zinn, Howard. *A People's History of the United States, 1492–Present.* New York: Harper Perennial Modern Classics, 2005.

Maps

Capon, Lester J., Barbara Bartz Petchenik, and John Hamilton Long. *Atlas of Early American History: The Revolutionary Era 1760–1790*. Princeton, NJ: Princeton University Press. 1976.

Schull, Nicolas. Map of Pennsylvania, commissioned by an act of Parliament for the Penn brothers, 1759. Copy at Mennonite Heritage Center, Harleysville, PA.

The Author

Ervin R. Stutzman was born into an Amish home in Kalona, Iowa, and spent most of his childhood in Hutchinson, Kansas. He serves as executive director for Mennonite Church USA and has also served the Mennonite church in the roles of pastor, district overseer, mission administrator, area conference moderator, seminary dean, and moderator of the denomination. He holds master's degrees from the University of Cincinnati and Eastern Mennonite Seminary, and received his PhD from Temple University.

Ervin's past publications include *Being God's People*, a study for new believers; *Creating Communities of the Kingdom* (coauthored with David Shenk); *Welcome!*, a book encouraging the church to welcome new members; *Tobias of the Amish*, a story of his father's life and community; *Emma, A Widow Among the Amish*, the story of his mother; and *From Nonresistance to Justice*, a book that examines the past hundred years of peacemaking in the Mennonite church. He has also published articles and contributed chapters to other books.

Ervin is married to Bonita Haldeman of Manheim, Pennsylvania. They live in Harrisonburg, Virginia, where they are members of Park View Mennonite Church. Ervin and Bonita have three adult children, Emma, Daniel, and Benjamin; and two grandchildren, Felix and Eva.

www.ingramcontent.com/pod-product-compliance
Lightning Source LLC
Chambersburg PA
CBHW070759050426
42452CB00012B/2404